BLIND VECTOR

C. ROBERT BEALE

BLIND VECTOR

C. ROBERT BEALE

Kravitz & Sons

INNOVATORS IN PUBLISHING, MARKETING AND ADVERTISING

Kravitz and Sons LLC
204 E Arlington Blvd. Suite B
Greenville, NC 27858

Published by Kravitz and Sons LLC.

ISBN: 979-8-89639-719-9 (sc)
ISBN: 979-8-89639-718-2 (e)

Dedication

This book is dedicated to my friend Dotty Blakely, formerly a fellow Rhode Island National Guard soldier, who convinced me that not trying to write this book would be worse than any rejections I suffered along the way. Thank you Dotty, wherever you are.

Table Of Contents

CHAPTER ONE

Threads of gold spread across the horizon, searing the darkness like a raging inferno. The blackness of the night dissipated as the magnificent hues of dawn filtered through the eastern sky. Orange and yellow bands of phosphorescent light painted the low-flying clouds.

The windsock on the control tower roof hung limply from its mast. In the distance Chesapeake Bay lay placid, motionless as if it were a large piece of turquoise glass.

Suddenly the early morning silence was shattered by the sound of jet engines being started. They made an ear-piercing, whirring sound, which soon became a powerful roar. A single jet aircraft taxied away from the aircraft parking area, its strobe lights flashing and bluish-yellow flames spewing from its exhaust ports. The plane, an older model A-3, had entered service in the mid 1950's and was one of the few remaining in the Navy. It was also the heaviest aircraft ever flown from an aircraft carrier. Its primary function for most of its service life had been as an electronic warfare platform although it had sometimes been used as a mid-air refueling tanker. They were being replaced by the newer EA-6B Prowlers, which were faster, and more maneuverable. This A-3 carried a crew of five rather than a crew of seven because it had a pressurized compartment in the former weapons bay for three Electronic Counter Measures operators as well as various sensors. Some early models also had tail guns, but these had been replaced with an electronic counter measures tail; it was nicknamed "The Whale". The EA-3B was usually assigned to fleet reconnaissance squadrons such as VAQ-47.

The A-3 glistened in the morning sun. Its white fuselage and silver tipped wings reflected the brilliant light of the new dawn. On the side of the plane, just below the cockpit, was the squadron's crest a globe with a large clenched fist protruding from the center of it. In the fist, a pair of yellow lightning bolts. On the tail, the large block letters AP were emblazoned in red with black trim, giving them a three-dimensional appearance. At the tip of the tail the number 730 was painted in four inch black digits.

Commander Charlie Boyle sat at the controls. He was a career naval officer, he had come from a long line of naval officers; his father, grandfather, and great-grandfather had been in the Navy. His father, in World War II, had commanded a battleship until December 7, 1941 when he was killed by a Japanese suicide pilot. His grandfather in was in World War I and had commanded a destroyer; his great-grandfather had sailed with John Paul Jones during the American Revolution. Charlie had graduated in the top twenty of his class at Annapolis; and dreamed, one day, of flying the Space Shuttle into outer space. He was just five feet eight inches tall, one hundred and seventy-five pounds. He had light brown hair with just a touch of gray at the temples. He wore an orange flight suit, a green survival gear vest, and a bright yellow inflatable life preserver. He had a pearl-handled thirty-eight-caliber revolver in a shoulder holster under his left arm. His oxygen mask dangled from a catch on the right side of his helmet.

The co-pilot was Lieutenant Commander James Johnston, a tall slender man; six feet two inches tall, one hundred fifty pounds. His cleanshaven face made him look much younger than his forty-two years. A thin scar curved its way from the bottom of his lip to the right side of his chin. It was a silent reminder of his two years as a prisoner of the North Vietnamese at the Hoa Loa Prison; the conditions there were miserable, and the food so bad that the prison was sarcastically nicknamed the "Hanoi Hilton" by the inmates, because it surely wasn't one of the well-known and upscale Hilton Hotels. He still suffered from nightmares from his time there; in spite of several years' worth of Post Traumatic Stress counseling. He also had on an orange flight suit, a green survival vest, and a bright yellow inflatable life preserver; his oxygen mask hung from a catch on the left side of his helmet. He carried a nine millimeter Beretta in a shoulder holster under his left arm.

Seated in the rear pressurized compartment in the former weapons bay was Aviation Electronics Technician Third Class Joe "Sparks" Greene. Sparks, as he was called by most of the people who knew him, was only twenty-three. He had graduated from the Derby Electronics Institute at fifteen years old. He was so good at electronics that he had been offered a number of jobs outside of the service that paid much better salaries than he could ever make in the Navy but, he wanted to serve his country. What he really wanted was to be a naval aviator but his eyesight was only marginal at best, with glasses, so that dream would never come true; he figured being a member of the aircrew was a suitable second choice. None of the three were married or even romantically involved at the present time.

Once the twin Pratt & Whitney J57 turbojet engines were turning and up to operating temperature; Boyle followed the blue runway lights to the end of runway Two-Left. When they reached the end of the runway Boyle turned right and applied the brakes.

"Oceania tower, this is Alpha-Papa-Seven-Three-Zero, over," Boyle said, holding his oxygen mask to his face and speaking into the built-in microphone.

"This is Oceania, go ahead Seven-Three-Zero."

"Oceania, this is Seven-Three-Zero, request clearance for take-off on runway Two-left, over."

"Roger, Seven-Three-Zero. You are cleared for immediate take-off. Have a good flight, Commander."

Boyle held the control stick with his left hand and reached for the throttle levers with his right. Cupping his hand over both knobs and hooking his thumb under them for a firm grip, he pushed them steadily forward.

As the plane rolled down the runway, picking up speed, Johnston reached up with his left hand and flipped a switch marked "Afterburner". A giant yellow fireball shot out of the back of each of the twin engines. The additional thrust catapulted the plane into the air.

Johnston turned off the afterburners and then flipped another switch to retract the landing gear while Boyle piloted the plane to its cruising altitude of five thousand feet. When their course was set, due east, and the air speed was set, Boyle called to Sparks on the intercom.

"Okay, Sparks, switch on the jammers."

"Aye, aye sir," the young man replied.

Sparks turned on the power switches and watched as the green indicator lights flickered and the various meters began to show that the equipment was working. There were three radar jamming units on board that would cause false signals, sometimes called ghosting, on the enemy's radar screen. By projecting many false targets it would be very difficult for the enemy to locate a particular target in order to shoot it down. It was usually pretty effective.

"Jammers are operational, skipper. I have them set for all frequencies, sir."

"Good work, Sparks."

They flew due east for thirty minutes at five thousand feet and then turned south and dropped down to five hundred feet. They continued for another ten minutes before sighting the ship, the U.S.S. John F. Kennedy, CVA 67. The Kennedy, or Big John as it was sometimes called, was a non-nuclear powered aircraft carrier; its purpose was strictly an air combat platform. It typically carried eighty or more aircraft, depending on the type of squadron and the size of the aircraft. It had been commissioned on September 7, 1968 and was home ported out of Norfolk Naval Base, Virginia. Its flight deck was over one thousand feet long and two hundred and fifty two feet wide at its widest point. The ship carried a crew of approximately five thousand when the air crews were aboard. There were thirty three airplanes on the flight deck; another forty seven were below in the hangar bay.

"This is the part I like, Jim. I love it when we can dump on those clowns. You'd better get back there and get our presents ready."

"Sure thing, skipper," Johnston replied excitedly, "this is going to be fun. I've got a bet with a friend of mine on that floating hotel. He doesn't think we can get in undetected."

Johnston unhooked his seat belt and slid out of his parachute harness. Disconnecting his oxygen hose and radio cord from the console, he made his way through the narrow companionway to the back of the plane.

When he reached the tail section, Johnston opened a small cupboard and took out two five-pound bags of flour. He placed them on the floor and closed the cupboard door. Beside his foot there was a small tube-like object which stood about sixteen inches high and was approximately five inches in diameter. Opening the cover on top of the cylinder, he dropped the flour sacks, one on top of the other, into the chamber. Then he waited for Boyle to signal him to press the release button.

Holding his oxygen mask to his face, Boyle radioed the ship.

"Big John, this is Navy Alpha-Papa-Seven-Three-Zero. How do you read me, over?"

"This is Big John; we read you Lima-Charley, Seven-Three-Zero. What can we do for you, over?"

"Big John, we are on a simulated attack run to check our electronic equipment and request your radar fix on us, over."

"Roger, Seven-Three-Zero, we have you on radar at two-five miles out, and an altitude of one-four-thousand feet, over."

Boyle laughed out loud as he signaled Johnston to drop their bombs.

"Negative, Big John, we're at five hundred feet directly over your head. I regret to inform you that your ship has been sunk, over and out."

As the A-3 peeled off to the left, Sparks looked out of the window and saw their flour sacks explode on top of the canopies of two of the aircraft parked on the carrier's flight deck. A cloud of white dust billowed along the deck, carried by the wind.

"Nice shooting, Mister Johnston; hope one of those was your friend's plane," Sparks said.

"Okay, Sparks, you can turn off the jammers. We're headed home."

"Aye, aye skipper," Sparks replied, switching off the power.

Boyle settled back in his seat, reached into his left breast pocket and took out a pack of Marlboros. He extracted a cigarette, put the pack back into his pocket and found his lighter. Lighting the cigarette, he sucked the smoke deep into his lungs.

"Flight surgeon says I should quit," he thought, as he slowly savored the flavor of the smoke, "but what the heck, a man's got to have at least one vice."

He closed the lighter and put it back into his pocket. He took another puff deep into his lungs and called to his men.

"The smoking lamp is lit, gentlemen," he said, exhaling the smoke.

Boyle finished his cigarette and crushed it out in the ashtray on the console beside him and thought about his schedule for the rest of the day.

"Debriefing when we land, monthly reports, quarterly reports, flight log. Nothing but paperwork; I spend more time flying a desk than I do flying a plane."

His thoughts were interrupted by Sparks' voice.

"Skipper, I was wondering if you would mind giving me a hand tomorrow? If you're free, I mean, sir."

"What's on your mind, Sparks?"

"Well, you see sir; I've been working on a remote control model airplane with a friend of mine. He's at sea right now," Sparks said, folding his chart table away into its compartment. "I've been trying to get the bugs out of the radio gear, testing it on the ground. I want to try it in the air, but I don't know how to fly it."

"So, what do you want me to do, give you some lessons," Boyle asked, glancing at the compass. He pushed the control stick to the left a little and made a slight change in their course.

"Well, actually I'd hoped that you would fly it for me. You see it's pretty big and I don't think I could learn enough."

"What kind of plane is it?"

"It's a jet-powered 747."

"Jet powered?"

"Oh, yes, sir. It's a completely scaled down version of a 747. It's about nine feet long with an eight foot wing span and four jet engines."

"This I've got to see," Boyle said, casting a look of disbelief toward his co-pilot. "Where do you keep something that big?"

"It's in my garage, skipper."

"Well, I'd really like to take a look at it, Sparks, but I don't know about flying it. I've never flown a model that big before. You'd be taking a big chance with your plane."

"Don't worry, skipper. I'm sure that if you had an accident with it, I could fix it. I'm just afraid that if I did it there wouldn't be anything left. I've lost a couple of smaller planes that I built by not having someone else pilot them."

"Skipper, we're less than five miles from touchdown," Johnston interrupted, "shall I begin the landing checklist?"

"Yes, Jim. We'll finish this discussion on the ground, Sparks," Boyle said, reaching for his oxygen mask.

"Oceania tower, this is Alpha-Papa-Seven-Three-Zero, request landing instructions, over."

"Seven-Three-Zero, this is Oceania tower. You are cleared for landing on runway two right. The wind is from the east at five knots, over."

"Roger, Oceania, Alpha-Papa-Seven-Three-Zero, out."

Boyle flipped the switch to lower the landing gear. The doors of the gear housing dropped open and the wheels came down. The familiar whine of the hydraulic system lowering them was followed by a solid thump.

"Give me forty percent flaps, Jim," Boyle said looking at the wheel lock indicator which flickered once and then illuminated brightly.

"Aye, aye, skipper, forty percent."

Johnston threw the switch and looked out of the cockpit window to watch the flaps as they began to descend from the back of the wings. Once they were in position, he released the switch.

"Forty percent flaps, aye, skipper."

The end of the runway was now in sight and Boyle eased the control stick forward a little. Pulling back on the throttle levers, he slowed their air speed down to one hundred and fifty knots. The big plane touched down smoothly and taxied to the aircraft parking area. The three men turned off the various switches, lights, and meters and left the plane.

Once their debriefing was finished, they decided to drive to Sparks' home and look at the model. Sparks led the way. He drove out the main gate and turned left onto the long, barren stretch of road that led to the highway.

When they reached the end of the access road, Sparks turned right and headed for a small housing development. He drove about three miles and turned left onto Cobbs Street. Cobbs went through the center of the housing complex. There were a few short cul-de-sacs on either side of Cobbs. Each was lined with identical, redbrick, ranch type homes.

Sparks drove down Cobbs until he reached Andrea Lane. It was a pleasant street, lined with dwarf cherry trees and small brick homes. The lawns were thick and lush, like a green deep-piled carpet.

Sparks turned into the driveway of one of the brick homes. He and another Radioman on the base shared the house. They liked it a lot better than living on the base. It wasn't a fancy place; it had two bedrooms, a living room, and a kitchen. A one-car garage sat about twenty feet behind the house. Sparks turned off the ignition and got out. The two officers pulled up behind him and got out.

The three men went directly to the garage. Sparks unlocked the door and then opened it. Boyle's eyes lit up brightly when he saw the inside of the garage. There, filling up most of the floor space sat the jetliner. It was just as Sparks had described it. The fuselage was about nine feet long and painted to look like a Transworld Airways passenger liner. The wings were disconnected and laying on a pallet to the left of the fuselage.

"It's beautiful, Sparks," Johnston exclaimed.

"Just look at the detail, Jim" Boyle added, kneeling beside the model.

"Thank you, sir," Sparks grinned, "I've tried very hard to make it as close to a real 747, as possible. Everything works too. It has interior lights, working cargo and passenger doors, and remote controlled starters for the engines. Everything is operated from the control box. I've got that locked up in the house."

"Sparks, where were you planning to fly this thing? For that matter, how were you planning on getting it out of this garage," Johnston queried.

"Well, you see, sir…with the wings detached, we'll load it onto a small trailer that I built for transporting it. The wings are held in mounts on either side of the trailer. I made arrangements to use an old, abandoned airport about ten minutes from here. It's pretty isolated there and we won't have to worry about disturbing anyone with the noise and there is plenty of room to maneuver."

Standing to his feet, Boyle said, "looks like you've thought everything out pretty well."

"Well, we've certainly tried to plan for every contingency, skipper. After all, this has been a four year project."

"Four years," Johnston exclaimed, arching his eyebrows in surprise. "Do you mean to say that you've been working on this thing for four years?"

"Yes, sir, Bill and I have put four years and about three thousand dollars into this project. That's why I'm so anxious to see her in the air."

"Well, Sparks, I'll tell you what," Boyle said, glancing at his Rolex, "I have the day off tomorrow and I'd be willing to see what we can do to help you realize that dream if you still want me to."

"All right," Sparks yelped.

"Jim. Do you want to join us," Boyle questioned.

"Are you kidding, skipper? I wouldn't miss it for anything." "Okay then, what do you say we meet here at 0700?"

The men agreed and the two officers left.

CHAPTER TWO

By five o'clock in the morning, Sparks was up, showered, shaved and ready to go. He made a pot of coffee and went to work loading the wings and fuselage onto the trailer. He was loading the radio transmitter and a toolbox when the two officers arrived.

"Good morning, Sparks," Boyle said, walking up the driveway.

"Good morning, skipper; you too Mister Johnston."

"What can we do to help you get ready, Sparks," Johnston asked.

"Nothing, sir, I've got it all loaded and ready to roll."

"Well, let's do it then," Boyle said.

The three men got into Sparks' Camaro and drove away. Sparks headed for Cobbs Street and took a right. He drove about three miles and turned left and drove for another ten minutes until they reached an old dirt road. Turning into the dirt road, Sparks drove very slowly. They passed under an old pine tree that had most of its lower branches cut off and then turned right.

"They had to chop the branches off of that one a few years ago when they tried to get in here to remove some of the old planes," he told the officers.

After driving about three hundred yards further, Sparks braked beside a pile of weather beaten lumber and rusted corrugated iron. The airfield was large and barren; the only vegetation was some tall grass and weeds. What appeared to have been a dirt runway ran down the center of the large field.

"This is it, gentlemen, all that's left of a once proud little airport. That," he sighed, pointing to the pile of rubble, "that's what is left of the first hangar in Virginia to house a Jenny. This place used to be the Oceania Flight Training Base, back in World War I."

"The Jenny is a great little plane to learn to fly on," Johnston interjected, "when I was fifteen I bought one at an auction for fifty bucks. It was still in the original crate from the factory and I had to put it together before I could learn to fly it."

"Wow, really," Sparks asked.

"Yes, it was so much fun that I could never part with it. I still have it as a matter of fact. It is sitting in my mother's back yard in Indiana."

"How hard was it to learn to fly," Sparks asked, his eyes beaming.

"It was really simple, Sparks, it is a twin-seat biplane. The student sits in front of the instructor and both have controls. It was ideal for initial pilot training because its top speed was only seventy-five miles an hour and it was airborne at forty-five, it practically flew itself."

"Golly, I wish I could learn to fly," Sparks said, "It's been my dream since I was about ten years old.

The three men went to work and unloaded the plane. Johnston and Boyle mounted the wings as Sparks set up the transmitter; the big moment had finally come. The three men had a sense of excitement, much like that of a child on Christmas morning. They pushed the model into the center of the dirt runway and stopped.

"I'll show you the controls and how they work, skipper," Sparks said, switching on the power pack. "You can run through the ground tests I've been doing before taking off if you want, sir."

Boyle and Johnston watched intently as Sparks explained each of the control systems.

"These four switches are the engine pre-heaters. These are the throttle controls; you can set them individually or together, if you flip this little arm down. These two buttons are for the brakes. The white switch is for the interior lights and the blue one is for the cargo bay lights. This switch opens and closes the passenger doors and the next one is for the cargo door. The stick is for rudder and aileron control."

"You've got almost as many controls on this box as they do in the real cockpit, Sparks," Boyle's brow furrowed in amazement.

Sparks handed him the control box, "Well, Skipper, she's ready to go whenever you are."

Boyle pressed the button to turn on the interior lights. His eyes lit up almost as brightly as the lights inside of the plane. He opened and closed the doors. He tried the rudder and aileron controls. Seeing that they all worked he flipped the switches for the engine pre-heaters and the pushed the starter button for the first engine. It gave a loud whirring sound as the turbine started to turn and then, as it started to run, it emitted a thundering roar.

Boyle locked the brakes on all of the wheels and then started the remaining three engines. When all four engines had smoothed out he released the brakes and eased the throttles forward and allowed the plane to roll slowly toward the end of the old runway. He taxied the plane in a straight line for a short distance and then tuned it first to the left and then to the right. As the big model rolled toward the take-off point, Johnston and Boyle began to grin like Sparks had the night before. A gleam in their eyes as if they were just about to have their first ice cream cone.

"Well, Sparks," Boyle shouted over the roar, "let's see what she'll do."

Boyle taxied the plane to the end of the runway and turned it into the wind. Holding the brakes firmly, he pushed the throttle levers all the way forward. The big model shuddered under the thrust of the four jet engines. As he released the brakes, the plane lurched forward and picked up speed. When the nose wheels lifted off of the ground, a cheer of jubilation went up from Sparks and Johnston. The model climbed smoothly to an altitude of about thirty feet. Boyle pressed another button and the wheels folded neatly into their compartments and the doors closed. As Boyle moved the aileron and rudder controls, the plane responded instantly and banked into a large sweeping circle around the field. He flew it in a gradually increasing circle of the field several times and then brought it in closer to prepare for landing.

"So much for the easy part, Sparks," he said, aligning the nose of the

plane with the end of the runway. "The test of any good pilot is whether or not he can land without killing himself."

As the plane side-slipped, buffeted by the wind, Boyle pressed the button to lower the landing gear. Nothing happened! He pressed it again. But there was still no response.

"Sparks," He shrieked, "the wheels won't come down. I'll circle the field; see what's wrong.

Pushing the throttles forward again, Boyle put the plane into a large, lazy circle around the field. Once it was flying level, he handed the control box to Sparks. Sparks tried the control for the wheels but nothing happened.

"I've never tested them before because I didn't have any way to hold it up."

Sparks took a screwdriver and opened the back of the control box. Pushing through the spaghetti-like maze of multi-colored wires, he looked at the components that were mounted on the main processor-control board.

"Looks like a shorted diode, it's keeping the relays from energizing."

He removed a pair of cutting pliers from a small leather pouch in the toolbox. Reaching into the control box, he snipped one of the leads on the faulty component.

"Come on, baby" he said tensely as he pushed the button again. The doors dropped open and the landing gear fell into place.

"Thank God," Boyle sighed heavily when he saw the wheels come down. Sparks handed him the control box and Boyle brought the plane in for a landing. The model landed smoothly like a graceful eagle in the grassy field. The three men breathed a collective sigh of relief.

Johnston was the first to speak, "Nice job, Skipper, you're a cinch to get a job with American when you retire."

"Yeah, that was great, Skipper," Sparks echoed.

"Thanks guys," Boyle said turning off the power pack, "but the real credit goes to you Sparks, for the fast work on that landing gear."

"I'll fix that when I get home. Then I'm going to put her up on blocks and test it out before she goes in the air again. Anything else I should do, skipper?"

"No, Sparks. I think that with the landing gear problem solved you'll have it all. I'd be happy to fly it again for you any time."

The three men took the wings off of the fuselage and loaded everything onto the trailer. Once everything was in place and they were in the car headed back toward Sparks' house, Johnston spoke, "You know, skipper, I think we all deserve a drink and with your permission I'd like to buy the first round. I've got a couple of things to celebrate, the maiden flight of Alpha-Papa-Seven-Three-Zero-Junior and the bet I won yesterday."

"You're on, Jim" Boyle replied with a grin. Sparks nodded in cheerful agreement.

"Great then, as soon as we get this baby back in the barn, we'll head for the mountains."

When they arrived back at Sparks' house, they parked the trailer, unloaded the cargo, and locked it up in the garage. Once everything was secure, they drove to a small bar located about ten miles from the Naval Base. The name on the front read "The Bar".

"The Bar" was not very elaborate, but it was comfortable. The chairs were the old-fashioned, straight-backed kind; the tables tended to wobble. A well-worn jukebox stood in a corner next to the wall; on the wall hung dart board. A pool table took up much of the floor. The bartender was a friendly sort of man, not too over-bearing, but at the same time a person who commanded respect in his own right.

Boyle ordered a scotch-and-soda, Johnston a rum-and-coke, and Sparks a bourbon-and-water. When the drinks came, Johnston pulled out a fifty-dollar bill and gave it to the bartender.

"Keep 'em coming as long as this lasts," he said, "this party is on Lieutenant JG Wally Lewis of the U.S.S. John F. Kennedy. He's the schmuck whose airplane we bombed yesterday."

"Be sure to thank the good Lieutenant for us, Jim" Boyle said, lifting his glass in a toast.

Boyle sipped the scotch. The smoky taste sent a shiver of pleasure through his tired nerves.

Johnston drank down half of his Bacardi's in one gulp. Placing the glass on the table, he reached into his pocket and took out his pipe, a rather large Graybow. Putting the stem in his mouth, he held a match to the bowl and spoke, as he puffed, "Not too sure I can do that, skipper, Old Wally wasn't very happy when he paid me last night…especially since his canopy was open when the flour sack hit the top of his windshield."

The three men roared with laughter. When the laughter subsided the conversation turned to the day's events.

"Sparks," Boyle began, "I really can't get over the amount of work you've put into that model airplane; the detail is just incredible. Why, you've even got the correct livery on the fuselage."

"You bet, skipper," Sparks replied, "it's taken a lot of time and effort, but seeing it in the air today made it all worth while."

"You know, Sparks," Johnston interjected, "what I can't get over is how fast you isolated that problem with the controls. You're really a genius with that electronics stuff, aren't you?"

"Well, I'd hate to think of what would've happened if he weren't a genius, Jim," Boyle added.

Besides even after the three years, ten months, and sixteen days that the three of us have been together as a crew this young man still impresses me.

"To you, Sparks," Boyle said raising his glass in a toast. The three drained their glasses on the toast.

By nine-thirty, they were really feeling the effects of the alcohol, especially Johnston.

"You know something, Sparks," Johnston began, in a muffled tone, "that model of yours has given me a brilliant idea. What if someone got a hold of some equipment like yours and put it in a real plane? He could probably hijack a jetliner if he had the inclination.

"Awe Jim, I think you've had too much to drink," Boyle cautioned, "the idea is absurd. If I didn't know you I'd think you were serious."

"Actually, skipper, he has a good point there. Bill and I have been thinking about doing something similar to that. Imagine a remote-controlled cargo plane for carrying hazardous cargo, or for evacuating wounded from a combat zone without having to risk the lives of other people."

"Yeah…and if there were remote-controlled bombers or spy planes people like me wouldn't get shot down and have to rot for years in Commie prison camps," Johnston added somberly.

"I guess you do have a valid point there," Boyle replied, toying with his glass, "but, the idea of hijacking a plane by remote-control is preposterous. You'd better hope that no one from Naval Criminal Investigative Services hears you talking like that, they'd lock you up and throw away the key."

"Maybe you're right, skipper, but the idea is intriguing just the same," Johnston said.

"Come on, let's get out of here, Jim," Boyle said standing to his feet. "I think we've all had enough, besides I'm hungry. Let's go somewhere and get a steak, my treat."""

Sparks helped Boyle steer Johnston out of the bar and into the car. An idea was beginning to take shape in his mind, and he pondered it silently.

"What if someone could hijack a plane by remote-control," he thought, "no one would be able to catch him. Commercial air travel wouldn't be safe."

The thought disturbed Sparks. Yet, he found it a fascinating challenge at the same time.

The three men drove to a Longhorn Steakhouse for dinner. The next morning dawned bright and clear, the base weather report called for another perfect day. At the morning briefing, Captain John Clarion a tall, blonde haired, forty-five year old man told Boyle and his crew to remain after the briefing, he wanted to speak to them privately.

Once the other aircrews had cleared the ready room, Captain Clarion turned to Boyle and said, "You're little joke on the Kennedy the other day was not appreciated by the ship's captain,

Mister. The admiral has forwarded a formal letter of reprimand, which will be placed in your permanent records. As for you, personally, Boyle, this incident will probably cost you your promotion to captain. Look, you men, I don't mind a little fun once in a while; but that was a darn stupid thing to do," Clarion struggled to control his temper, "that is not, however, the main reason I wanted to talk to you men," pulling a sheet of paper out of a brown loose-leaf binder. "You men are being reassigned to a California squadron for temporary duty. I'm sending you out there, not because of this incident but, because you men are the best electronic counter measures team I have and because none of you are married. The admiral has ordered me to send a top-notch flight crew to help train other crews in electronic warfare. You'll be there for about a year. Everything you own will be shipped, at Navy expense, if you want to take it with you."

"Have we nothing to say in the matter, sir," Boyle asked quietly.

"No, you don't. This is the Navy, commander, we go where we are ordered to go and do what we are ordered to do. The paperwork is being processed. You have one week to pack. You'll fly out there Monday morning and your belongings will arrive on Tuesday afternoon."

"Sir, what about housing when we get there," Johnston asked.

"The squadron will provide you with quarters, or you can look for something off-base on your own time."

"Sir, I'd like permission to fly out there tomorrow to look for some off-base housing," Boyle said, casting a sympathetic glance at his crewmen.

"Granted, that is all."

The three men saluted, then left the ready room and walked silently to their plane.

When the pre-flight checklist was completed, Boyle radioed the tower for take-off instructions. "Oceania tower this is Alpha-Papa-Seven-Three-Zero, request clearance for take-off, over."

"Roger, Seven-Three-Zero," the radio crackled, "you are cleared for take-off on runway two-left. Proceed when ready, over."

"Thank you, Oceania, Alpha-Papa-Seven-Three-Zero, out."

Pushing the throttle levers forward with one hand, Boyle got a firm grip on the control stick. The A-3 roared down the runway and took to the air as effortlessly as always.

Sparks was the first to speak, "you know Mister Johnston, I was thinking about what you said, last night at the bar; about taking control of a plane by remote-control and hijacking it."

"Awe, come on Sparks, let's don't get him going on that again," Boyle said, frowning at the radioman.

"Why, what did I say that was so bad, skipper," Johnston asked, coyly.

"You had an idea about using my radio gear to hijack a real plane. Just for the fun of it I ran some numbers last night and I figure it really could be done, sir," Sparks added.

"Well, I suppose it could be possible, couldn't it," Johnston asked. "I would think it would be possible, but highly improbable," Boyle snapped. "You'd have to have some long range radio gear. Then you'd have the problem of gaining control of the plane and keeping it."

"I was thinking about that last night. Most commercial pilots switch to automatic pilot when they get to cruising altitude, don't they, skipper," Sparks queried.

"Well...yes, Sparks, a good many of them do. Especially on cross-country or transoceanic flights," the pilot replied, wondering where this conversation was headed.

Sparks' grin seemed to fill the lower half of his helmet, "There you have it, sir. When the pilot switches to the auto-pilot, it triggers a small explosive charge which disables the manual controls, and then you just use the radio-control device to fly the aircraft."

"And just how, may I ask, do you keep the plane from exploding when you detonate the charge? You'll have to come up with a better idea than that one, Sparks. While you are thinking about one though, I'd appreciate it if you'd keep the whole matter to yourself. It's dangerous to think things like that out loud," Boyle smirked.

That was the end of the conversation, as far as Boyle was concerned. His crewmen now began to get the equipment ready for the day's mission—a mock search and destroy raid on a single ship. Of course, this time there would be no flour sacks. Their target was a Fletcher-Class destroyer, following the carrier task force that was operating in the same region as the Kennedy.

"Sparks, switch on the jammers, and then keep an eye on our own radar," Boyle said, studying the digital NAVCOMP display. "I want you to jam all frequencies except our own. Set the range for three hundred miles, that way they won't even know we're in town until we're right on top of them."

"Aye, aye, sir," Sparks replied, flipping the switches before him.

As they neared the ship, Boyle radioed the destroyer captain. "Johnny Moe, this is Alpha-Papa-Seven-Three-Zero, do you read me, over?" Boyle said, lifting his mask to his face.

"We read you loud and clear, Seven-Three-Zero. What can we do for you, over?"

"Johnny Moe, this is Seven-Three-Zero. We are your friendly neighborhood radar blip looking for a home—can you tell us where we are, over?"

Static spattered in his earphones for several seconds, and then the voice came back on. "Seven-Three-Zero, we have you on radar at thirty-three miles and an altitude of three five thousand feet, over."

"That's not bad, Johnny Moe, except that we just dropped a thousand-pounder down your stack from three hundred feet, Over and out."

"Boyle gave a thumbs-up signal to Sparks to show his satisfaction. Once again they had done a very good job of fooling the "enemy" radar.

"If we ever do go to war again, I'm certainly glad that nobody has gotten close to our actual position when we've done this in training. It'd be pretty hard to shoot us down if they don't know where we are," Sparks said.

"Yeah, if I'd had this equipment in Nam I wouldn't have spent time in the Hanoi Hilton," Johnston said morosely.

"How'd they get you, Mister Johnston," Sparks pressed forward eagerly.

"I was on my first combat mission, over Hanoi. Back in 1966, I was flying an A-4 Skyhawk off the Ticonderoga on a Rolling Thunder raid. I had to go in low to drop napalm on Thunder Ridge; a SAM took out my hydraulic system and I had to eject. By the time I got to the ground there were about a hundred gooks waiting for me. Heck, I never had a chance."

"Heck, Mister Johnston, it's a miracle you're still alive. I heard that a lot of our pilots died in those camps."

"Yeah, it was really bad. I still dream about it once in a while."
"You can shut down back there, Sparks," Boyle interjected.

"Aye, aye, sir," Sparks replied, flipping all of the switches off. He watched as the lights faded and the meters dropped.

Once they had landed, Boyle and his crew went to debriefing and filled out the post-flight reports. When this was done, Boyle called the other two together.

"I've filed a flight plan to take Seven-Three-Zero to California tomorrow. I'm going to look for some off-base housing. I'd appreciate it if you'd join me; you don't have to, but it would make the trip a little easier."

"Sure thing, skipper," Johnston replied unzipping his flight suit.

"What time do we leave, sir?" Sparks asked.

"We're cleared for six-thirty take-off so pre-flight will begin at five-thirty. See you both then."

CHAPTER THREE

Five-thirty came early for Sparks; he was worried about the big model and what he should do with it. Bill would be at sea for several more months. At last, he decided to take the model to California; sublease the house; and write to Bill, telling him what had happened.

Boyle was going through his pre-flight checklist when Sparks and Johnston arrived at the airfield.

"Good morning, men," Boyle said, returning their salutes, "ready for our first transcontinental flight together?"

"Yes sir, skipper," Sparks answered.

"I'm all set. How's the bird looking today, skipper," Johnston asked. "The bird is fine and so is the weather, Jim. We've got a little bit of a storm out over Oklahoma. We'll be flying at thirty thousand though, so we should miss most of it."

"What do you estimate our flying time will be, skipper," Sparks asked.

"Well, our airspeed will be six hundred knots; I figure we'll have about five hours in the air, unless we have to stop for fuel. If we don't run into any problems with the weather or a strong head wind we've got enough fuel for six hours. I want to try to make it without stopping. If we need to stop, there's an Air Force base in Arizona."

The pre-flight checklist completed, the three men took their seats and got ready for take-off.

The ground crew chief gave Boyle the signal to start his engines. With a loud whirring sound, the turbines started to turn. Soon they were turning at normal speed, making a loud roar. Boyle radioed the tower for final clearance as Johnston checked the instruments. Sparks was busy in the back, setting the radios on the appropriate frequencies. They performed their normal duties with utmost efficiency, resembling the figurines of a finely tuned Swiss clock.

As the A-3 taxied to the end of runway two for take-off, the morning sun broke through the dawn. An orange ball of fire consumed the last fragments of the night and illuminated the cloudless sky with a brilliant display of color.

Boyle put the craft into a gradual climbing turn to the left. They quickly reached thirty thousand feet and headed due west.

Once they had achieved level flight, Boyle set their speed at six hundred knots. Then he called Sparks forward.

"Sparks, how would you like to take the controls for a while and get a feel for what it is like to fly this baby?"

Sparks' eyes beamed, his jaw gaping in surprise.

"Would I ever? Skipper, I've always wanted to fly in the co-pilot's position. I'm fascinated whenever I watch you or Mister Johnston at the controls. I've never thought I would have a chance to do it."

"Okay, Sparks, switch places with Jim; you're my new co-pilot for today."

Sparks stepped back, to allow Johnston to get out of his seat and move towards the rear of the plane. Then, he sat down in the co-pilot's seat and plugged his headphones and oxygen hose into the console. Meanwhile, Johnston made his way back to the radio compartment and sat down in Sparks' place.

Boyle put the main control of the aircraft onto the automatic pilot. He showed Sparks the locations of different controls and indicators, the dials and knobs, buttons and switches. He pointed to the altimeter and the turn-and-bank indicator, also known as the artificial horizon—a device that tells if the plane is flying level or not. He also pointed out the airspeed indicator and the compass.

"Turn that one to the right a little, Sparks."

With a nervous hand, Sparks took the knob and gave it a gentle turn. The right wing dipped as the plane turned to the right.

"Bring it back to the left now and watch the artificial horizon. Stop when we're level again. Put us back on course two-seven-zero."

Once Sparks had the plane back on course, Boyle showed him another knob. This one was more like a wheel than a knob. Only a small portion of it was exposed.

"This one is used to control our altitude," Boyle said, "if you turn it forward, we'll climb. If you turn it backward, we'll dive. Try a slow climb and watch your altimeter; level off when you get to thirty-three thousand feet."

"This is fantastic, skipper. Such a feeling of power when you do something so minor and the plane does so much."

"Yeah, Sparks, there is no greater feeling than when you sit behind these controls and put this baby through its paces. It's a lot like I felt the other day flying your model."

"Skipper, would it be all right if I took a few turns with the ship now?"

"Well okay, I'll tell you what; I'll have Johnston track a radar signal like you do when we're on a target run. When he gives you the course, turn towards it. Is that okay with you, Jim?"

"Sure thing, skipper."

"Okay, Sparks, it's your airplane."

"Yes sir, skipper," Sparks replied excitedly.

"Okay, Sparks, come left ten degrees," Johnston called over the intercom. "Aye, aye sir, left ten degrees," Sparks replied, turning the black knob. He watched the compass and the turn and bank indicator and leveled off once they reached the course. He corrected their altitude to maintain thirty-three thousand feet.

"That was fine, Sparks," Boyle said, pleased with the kid's natural aptitude.

"Sparks, now bring us around to the right three degrees," Johnston called once again.

Sparks put the plane into a slow—sweeping turn and stopped at the desired course."

"What's the target, Jim," Boyle asked.

"It's a small weather station, skipper."

"Okay Sparks, let me take over and put us back on course for California. I'll let you try it again sometime when we're out over the water and there is less of a chance of a mid-air collision."

"That's great, skipper, thanks for the opportunity. This has to be the best flight I've ever had," Sparks said, sitting, back in the seat while Boyle took the controls.

Sparks stayed in the cockpit for the next couple of hours. Johnston took a nap in the radio room. There was considerably more room to stretch out back there.

When he awoke, Johnston went forward to the cockpit and exchanged places with Sparks. Upon plugging into the intercom, he began relating a dream that he'd just been having.

"It was really a strange dream," he said, shuddering at the memory. "It wasn't like any of the flashbacks I've had before. Usually, I'm the only one in them. I see myself being captured by the Viet Cong. This time though, all three of us were in it. We were jamming someone, then for some reason you radioed the base and told them that we were going to crash in the Pacific."

"Did we crash, sir," Sparks asked.

"I don't know," I woke up and realized that it was just a dream."

"Have you had dreams like this often, Jim," Boyle asked, his brow rose in concern.

"No, skipper. When I first got back from Nam I used to wake up two or three times a night in a cold sweat from flashbacks of being captured, but I've been taking medication and seeing a psychiatrist. I don't get them very often anymore.

"Well, when we get back to Virginia, maybe you should go to see him."

"Yes, sir, I might just do that. This isn't the only one I've had this week. Last night I dreamt that we pulled off that remote-controlled hijacking that we talked about the other day."

"How'd we do that," Sparks asked.

"I don't exactly know, we were just doing it. The skipper and I were in a semi, you weren't around."

"What were we doing in a semi, Jim," Boyle asked in disbelief.

"You were in the trailer, controlling the plane, and I was driving."

"I was controlling the plane? With what, Sparks' little box," Boyle queried skeptically, wondering in his own mind why he was letting Jim draw him into that discussion again.

"No, you were using a whole bunch of really sophisticated radio gear."

"That could explain today's dream, Mister Johnston," Sparks interjected. "What do you mean, Sparks?"

"Well, if we faked a crash, stole this plane and stripped it, all we would have to do is to put it into a truck and there you would have the two dreams combined."

"All right, I think that I've heard enough of this," Boyle interrupted. "it's not bad enough that you two are talking about a hijacking, now you want to steal a military plane too. The more you talk about this whole idea the crazier it gets. I would appreciate it if the both of you would just forget the whole thing."

"It's just a dream, skipper," Johnston argued.

"Yes, skipper, and if we analyze it we can find out what is going on in his sub-conscious mind. Maybe he could find a way to get rid of the dreams," Sparks said.

"You've got a good point there, Sparks," Boyle said, "but why don't we just leave the psychoanalyzing to the shrink."

"Yes sir," Sparks said.

"Jim, take over for a while, will you? Sparks, take my seat. I'm going back to stretch out for a little while."

"Sure thing, skipper."

Boyle went back to Sparks' seat and put his head down on the small chart table that Sparks used for his messages. The table sat directly below the jamming equipment power switches. Putting his head down on the table, Boyle tripped one of the switches with his helmet without realizing that it had happened.

Several minutes later, after Boyle had drifted off to sleep, the voice of a frantic air traffic controller came over the radio.

"Alpha-Papa-Seven-Three-Zero, this is Albuquerque tower, over!"

"This is Alpha-Papa-Seven-Three-Zero, go ahead Albuquerque, over," Johnston replied.

"Seven-Three-Zero, this is Albuquerque. Where are you, over?"

"Albuquerque, this is Seven-Three-Zero. Say again your last, over."

"Seven-Three-Zero, we've lost radar in all vectors! We are totally blind. We are trying to locate everyone we were tracking before the radar went out, and chart them on a wall graph. Please give us your present course, altitude, and airspeed, over."

"Sparks, get the skipper, please," Johnston said sharply, staring at Sparks in horror.

"Right away, sir," Sparks unfastened his seatbelt, grabbed his oxygen hose, and slipped out of his seat.

Johnston held his mask to his face, checking the gages, he radioed Albuquerque. "Albuquerque tower, this is Seven-Three-Zero. We are approximately two hundred miles due east of you, heading, west at a speed of six hundred knots, cruising altitude of three-three thousand, over."

"Roger, Seven-Three-Zero, we will be checking back with you in about five minutes. Keep your eyes open for two other aircraft, last seen on our radar, in your general vicinity. Both are heading west, over and out."

Johnston scanned the sky with his eyes. Three aircraft that close with no radar was a potential disaster. There was no sign of the other planes, but Johnston did see something that disturbed him. About five miles ahead, there raised a dark rampart of billowing clouds, the front Boyle had mentioned before they left Virginia. It was a lot higher than he had expected.

"Albuquerque tower, this is Alpha-Papa-Seven-Three -Zero, over." Johnston's palms suddenly sprouted sweat. He swallowed hard and raised the mask to his face.

The radio crackled, "This is Albuquerque, go ahead Seven-Three-Zero, over."

"Albuquerque, this is Seven-Three-Zero. No sign of other traffic but I am about to enter a very high layer of clouds; looks like a thunderstorm. Please advise, over."

The static in the headphones crackled once again, and then the voice from the tower replied. "Seven-Three-Zero, maintain present heading and speed. Hold altitude three-three thousand until we locate other traffic. We estimate that you are closing on a commercial "heavy" airliner. He should be two thousand feet below you, over."

"Roger, Albuquerque. This is Seven-Three-Zero, standing by." Sparks woke Boyle with the news as soon as he got back to the radio room. He spotted the switch that had been inadvertently turned on almost instantly.

"Skipper, I don't know how or when it happened," Sparks reported, "but one of us hit the power switch for one of the jammers and turned it on. That must be the cause of the radar problem they're having downstairs."

"You're probably right, Sparks; turn it off while I radio Albuquerque," Boyle said, standing to his feet.

As Boyle stood up to walk back to the cockpit, the right side of the plane dipped sharply. Both men were thrown violently against the side of the plane.

"What the heck is going on, Jim," Boyle screamed, scrambling to his feet again.

"We just missed being clobbered by a 747, skipper. In this storm I didn't see him until it was almost too late. He's supposed to be two-thousand feet below us."

"Better report it to Albuquerque, Jim." Boyle advised, taking his seat in the cockpit.

"Albuquerque tower, this is Alpha-Papa-Seven-Three-Zero, over," Johnston said nervously holding the mask to his face with his left hand.

"This is Albuquerque, go ahead Seven-Three-Zero, over," the transmission was crackling and popping from the lightning in the storm below.

"This is Seven-Three-Zero. We wish to report a near miss, with that heavy commercial traffic. He's at thirty-three thousand feet, on the same course as we were. We almost had a mid-air collision, over."

"Seven-Three-Zero, go up to four-zero thousand and await further instructions, over."

"Roger, Albuquerque, climbing to four-zero thousand now, over." Johnston pulled back on the stick, watching the altimeter. Boyle connected his radio cord and oxygen hose to the console.

"I'll take it now, Jim," he said. "Sparks, are you all right?"

"Yes, skipper, I'm all right. Just a little shaken," he shook his head vigorously.

"Get that switch turned off, will you?

"Yes sir," Sparks replied, reaching for the switch.

"Albuquerque tower, this is Alpha-Papa-Seven-Three-Zero, over." Boyle said, fastening his mask across his face.

"This is Albuquerque, go ahead Seven-Three-Zero, over."

"Albuquerque, we have just discovered a possible cause for your radar problem. How does it look now, over?"

After a pause of a few seconds, the voice returned, "Seven-Three-Zero, we've regained normal reception in all vectors. What in God's name happened up there, over?"

"Albuquerque, the exact information is classified, but I can tell you that we had a slight mishap in our radio room which caused the problem. We've corrected the problem and are very sorry for the mess it has caused you, over."

The operator's voice was sharp, "Are you sure this won't happen again, Seven-Three-Zero, over?"

"Affirmative, Albuquerque."

"We are going to need an incident report for the FAA, Seven-Three-Zero, over."

Great, just, great, Boyle thought, *an incident report will be sure to get me another official reprimand, which will make two in one week!*

"Roger, Albuquerque. What exactly do you need from me, over?"

"We need the pilot's full name, rank, and a detailed explanation, in writing, as soon as possible after you land, over."

"Roger, Albuquerque. Pilot's name is Charles Boyle, Commander, United States Navy. I will send a full report to the FAA immediately after landing at North Island Naval Air Station in San Diego, over."

"Roger, Seven-Three-Zero, thanks for the fast work in locating the problem. It really caused a panic down here. Have a good flight, over and out."

Boyle could tell from the sound of the air traffic controller's voice that he was truly relieved that the emergency was over. With a sinking heart, Boyle realized that he had not heard the last of this incident.

"Sparks, what happened back there," Johnston asked brusquely.

"I don't exactly know, sir," he said. "It looks like one of us bumped the power switch and turned on one of the jammers."

"How could that have happened," Johnston asked in a bewildered tone. "I have a hunch, but I have to try something to be sure," Sparks replied, turning to Boyle he asked.

"Skipper, when you went back to take your nap, did you put your head down on my table?"

"Yes, I did, Sparks, why?"

"Well it looks as though your helmet probably brushed the switch and turned on the jammer. I want to try it to prove my theory."

Putting his head on the table, Sparks heard the faint sound of a click. He quickly sat up and turned the switch off. He went to the cockpit and flashed the officers an awkward smile.

"Looks like I'm the guilty party then," Boyle added in an abashed tone.

"The thing that amazes me," Johnston began, "is that Albuquerque was two hundred miles away when they got wiped out! Only one jammer was on. Imagine what would've happened if they were all operating."

Boyle shuddered, "I don't even want to think about that! We've already announced our arrival in this part of the country a lot louder than I would've cared to."

"One thing's for sure though, skipper," Sparks spoke up. "If someone wanted to, they could cause an awful lot of problems with this stuff, and the folks on the ground would never know what hit them."

"That's for sure, Sparks, and it also adds credence to your translation of my two dreams and how they fit together," Johnston added.

"I thought I told you two to forget about that hijacking idea, Jim," Boyle snapped, angered by the remark.

Johnston and Sparks stared dumb-founded at the pilot. Neither of them had expected him to be so upset. All three men sat in silence for quite a while.

Finally, Boyle spoke. "Look, Jim, I'm sorry for flying off at the handle like that. It was unreasonable, I know."

"No problem, skipper. I'm sorry for bringing up the idea anyway. I imagine that, by now, you're pretty sick and tired of hearing about my fantasies."

"No Jim, that's not it. I'm just upset about this jamming incident. First, there was that reprimand for bombing the Kennedy, and now this. I'll probably never see another promotion for as long as I live."

"Why is that, skipper," Sparks queried.

"This incident will be considered a breach of security, even though I didn't tell them exactly how it happened. I'm still in trouble for telling them we were responsible. My career is going down the drain very rapidly."

"You know, Jim, I've never told anyone this," Boyle said sadly, "but my greatest desire was to be an astronaut. They only take command officers though. I was passed over last time. These two incidents will probably guarantee that I'll never get into the space program."

Boyle's reflection was interrupted by a radio call.

"Alpha-Papa-Seven-Three-Zero, this is Albuquerque tower, over."

"This is Seven-Three-Zero, go ahead Albuquerque, over."

"Seven-Three-Zero, we've just received a distress call from the pilot of a small plane that was traveling on the same heading as you. His message was garbled, but as best we can make out, he's gone down with engine trouble. We'd like you to keep a lookout for him, over."

"Roger, Albuquerque. I understand and will keep a lookout for him, over."

"Thank you, Seven-Three-Zero. This is Albuquerque, over and out."

"Well, at least that one isn't my fault," Boyle muttered bitterly.

CHAPTER FOUR

Boyle released the automatic pilot and took over manual control of the plane. He and Johnston scanned the horizon looking for telltale signs of the missing aircraft. They sighted nothing.

"I think we'll put down to refuel at Luke, Jim," Boyle said, pushing the stick forward slightly. I want to have enough gas, just in case anything else happens."

"You're probably right, skipper. That storm back there didn't help our fuel supply any."

Boyle radioed the Luke Air Force Base control tower for clearance to land. "Luke tower, this is Navy Alpha -Papa-Seven-Three-Zero, request permission to land, over."

"Navy Alpha-Papa-Seven-Three-Zero, this is Luke tower. What is the purpose of your landing request, over?"

"Luke tower, this is Seven-Three-Zero. We would like to refuel for the balance of our flight to California, over."

"Roger Seven-Three-Zero. Standby; over."

"What's, the problem, skipper," Sparks asked, "why did they say to standby instead of giving us permission to land?"

"The air-traffic controller is going to have to get permission from base operations before he can allow us to land," Johnston explained, checking the fuel gauges.

"Navy Alpha-Papa-Seven-Three-Zero, this is Luke tower, over."

Boyle loosened his seat belt, shifted in his seat and replied, "This is Seven-Three-Zero, go ahead Luke, over."

"Seven-Three-Zero, what is your final destination, over?"

"Luke, I am heading for the "North Island Naval Air Station in San Diego, California, over."

"Roger, Seven-Three-Zero, I understand. Your destination is San Diego. What is your fuel status, over?"

"I have fourteen hundred pounds, over."

"Roger! Seven-Three-Zero, please standby, over."

The radio was silent for a few moments. Then the voice of the air-traffic controller came through once again.

"Seven-Three-Zero you are cleared to land on runway nine. Turn to the left ten degrees for radar identification, over."

"Roger, Luke, turning left now, over," Boyle said, moving, the control stick to the left.

"Seven-Three-Zero, we have you on radar. You are twenty-five miles from touchdown. Turn right ten degrees, over."

"Roger, Luke. Turning now," Boyle eased the stick to starboard.

"That looks good, Seven-Three-Zero. Now turn left fifteen degrees and follow that heading to base, over."

Boyle followed the instructions the controller gave him. Within minutes

they had flown, the short distance to the Air Force base. Boyle and Johnston made preparations for landing. The wheels were lowered and the flaps also; seat belts were fastened and they were in position.

"Seven-Three-Zero this is Luke tower. You are cleared for immediate landing. There will be a blue truck at the far end of the runway to guide you to the refueling point once you have landed."

"Roger Luke, I understand, over."

Boyle saw the threshold of the runway in the sun-baked distance. Gradually, he pulled back on the throttle levers. Slowing the plane down to one hundred and thirty knots, he released them. He easily landed the A-3 on the ground and slowed to about five miles per hour. The blue truck sat idling at the end of the runway. It carried a large "FOLLOW ME" sign on the back. The vehicle led him to a refueling truck.

A ground crewman stood a short distance from the tanker. He held his hands over his head, directing Boyle to turn the plane to the left. The crewman crossed his arms, signaling the plane to stop. Finally, he moved his hand in a cutting motion across his throat, and Boyle shut down the engines. As soon as Boyle turned off the turbo-fans, the crewman walked over to the plane and plugged his headphones into the radio jack, on the underside of the A-3's nose.

"Welcome to Arizona, Commander," he said, holding a small microphone.

"Thank you, Airman." Boyle smiled as he hastily ran through his post-flight checklist.

"What can we do for you today?"

"Well, how about filling it up. Check the oil, the wipers, and the tires. Is there any place I can get a car wash?" Boyle jested, making a note of the landing in his flight log.

"No, sir, I'm afraid we're fresh out. We'll have you gassed up in no time, sir. If you and your crew would like to get out and stretch your legs; we have a snack bar right over there," he said, pointing to a small white building about three hundred yards away.

"Thanks a lot, we might just do that."

Turning to his crewmen he asked, "Would either of you like to visit the snack bar?"

"Yes, sir," Sparks said, "I could go for a cold drink."

"Sounds good to me too," Johnston replied, slipping out of his parachute harness.

"Let's go then," Boyle said, unbuckling his seat belt.

The three men got out of the plane and walked to the snack bar. It was very small inside, even smaller than it looked from outside. There were four vending machines against the wall. One had candy, another had coffee, the third had cold drinks, and the fourth was a dollar bill changer.

"They certainly believe in big snack bars out here, don't they, skipper," Johnston chided.

"Yeah, Jim, we'd better be careful that we don't get lost in here; they might never find us," the three men laughed.

"It sure feels good to get out and walk around," Sparks said.

"Yeah, I don't know how those airline pilots do it, sitting in the cockpit for hours everyday," Johnston said, stretching his arms, "it must really get monotonous."

"Well, I suppose you get used to it after a while, Jim. Fifty grand a year

certainly helps too," Boyle replied. They finished their cold drinks and headed back to the plane. By the time they reached the plane, the fuel truck was ready to pull away. A short, thin sergeant walked up to Boyle and, saluted him.

"I need your signature for the fuel, sir. Sign here, please," he said, handing Boyle a clipboard and pen.

"Certainly, sergeant and thank you for the fast and highly efficient service."

"Thank you, sir," his craggy face beamed with pleasure at the compliment, "we're always glad to be of assistance to the Navy. Have a good flight, sir."

Flashing Johnston a crisp salute, the sergeant climbed into the fuel truck and drove away.

The three men climbed into the A-3 and prepared for take-off.

"Next stop is sunny California," Boyle said, pulling the rear door closed behind him.

Once they were seated, had plugged in their headphones, and fastened their seatbelts, Boyle turned on the switches to start the engines.

A ground crewman, in front of the plane, gave the signal for Boyle to start the turbines spinning. With a loud whirring sound, the engines came to life. Soon they were turning at normal speed. The crewman removed the wooden chocks from in front of the wheels, saluted the pilot, and directed Boyle to follow the blue truck.

The truck led them to the end of the runway, then pulled off to the side, giving them room to pass.

Stowing the laminated card, which held the pre-flight checklist, beside him Boyle held his mask to his face.

"Luke tower, this is Alpha-Papa-Seven-Three-Zero; request clearance for take-off, over."

"Roger, Seven-Three-Zero. You are cleared for take-off when ready." "Thank you, tower, thanks for the fuel, over and out."

Boyle pushed both throttle levers all the way forward. The engines shrieked in unison. The A-3 vibrated as it roared down the runway, picking up speed as it went. The nose wheel lifted; and with a throaty blast the plane hurled into the air.

"I wonder what ever became of that small plane, skipper," Sparks said.

Boyle watched the airbase fall away beneath his cockpit window. "I don't know, Sparks, keep your eyes open though."

About twenty minutes after take-off Johnston spotted some smoke rising from the desert floor.

"Take a look over there, skipper," Johnston pointed to the pillar of smoke.

"I see it, Jim," Boyle replied, both hands on the stick, "looks like an oil fire."

"Yeah, or it could be gasoline."

"We'd better take a look. I'll drop down to five hundred feet."

Boyle eased back on the throttles and slowed their speed down to two hundred knots. He pushed the stick forward and then leveled off at five hundred feet.

Minutes later they passed over the source of the smoke. It was a small Cessna that had crashed, the wreckage was on fire.

Holding his mask to his face, Boyle radioed Phoenix to report the wreck. "Phoenix tower, this is Navy Alpha-Papa-Seven-Three-Zero, over."

"This is Phoenix Tower. Go ahead Seven-Three-Zero, over."

"Phoenix, we've spotted the wreckage of what appears to be a small plane, approximately eight-zero miles west of you; no immediate sign of survivors, over."

"Roger, Seven-Three-Zero that could be the one Albuquerque's been looking for. Can you see the registration numbers on the plane, over?"

"Negative, Phoenix. It's burning pretty fiercely, there's too much smoke, over."

"Roger, Seven-Three-Zero. Thank you for notifying us. We will send a rescue unit out immediately, over and out."

"Skipper, take a look over there," Sparks cried out, pointing to a small house and a barn about a half-mile from the wreck. "If anyone is alive, they might have gone there."

"That is a possibility, Sparks," Boyle replied, forcing the A-3's nose down. "I'll take it in a little closer, maybe we can spot someone."

Boyle took the plane down to two hundred feet; he pulled back on the throttles slightly, slowing them down to one hundred-eighty knots.

As they flew over the house, they didn't see any signs of life. There was, however, a long, hard-packed dirt road that appeared suitable for landing.

"I'm going to put down, Jim. We'll see if there is anyone in the house or the barn and see if we can get closer to the wreck. Better give me full flaps."

"Full flaps, aye" Johnston said, reaching for the switch.

Boyle landed the plane on the dirt road. The sun-baked surface was surprisingly smooth. Boyle taxied up to the front of the house. The three men got out of the plane and went to the front door. Boyle knocked on the door but there was no answer. Johnston went to one of the windows and looked in.

"Looks like nobody lives here, skipper; there's nothing inside but a bunch of boxes and some big lights."

The three men turned away from the house and jogged across the sun-parched ground, heading in the direction of the wrecked plane.

By the time they reached the wreck, there wasn't much left. The Cessna's wings and fuselage were a mass of black, burnt metal. There was no sign of the pilot or anyone else around.

"Well, it looks like there's nothing we can do here," Boyle said. "Let's get back to the plane."

Dusty and smelling of smoke, the three men trudged back to their own plane. Boyle taxied down the old road and then turned the plane's nose into the wind for take-off.

Once they were airborne again, Boyle spotted a large, weather-beaten barn, about a mile from the house. Boyle radioed Phoenix to report what they had seen.

The balance of the flight took less than an hour. The landing at the North Island Naval Airbase was smooth and flawless. The A-3 taxied to the host squadron's hangar, Boyle and his crew got their first look at their West Coast counterparts.

The host squadron was also using A-3's. The hangar looked just like the one they had left behind in Virginia. A large sign hung over the door; it had the squadron crest painted on it. The crest was a large circle, painted like a globe with bright yellow circles criss-crossing around it.

The ground crewman assigned to them held his hands over his head and crossed them at the wrist. Boyle applied the brakes. When the plane stopped, the crewman gave Boyle the signal to cut the engines. As Boyle shut down the turbo-fans, Johnston turned off the power and instrument switches.

Climbing out of the plane the three men walked around it looking for anything that might be wrong. By the time they finished, a navy blue, nineteen seventy-eight Ford, four-door sedan drove up to them. A young man got out, walked over to Boyle, and saluted.

"Good morning, Commander Boyle, sir," he said, with a slight southern drawl. "I've been sent to drive you and your crew to your quarters."

"Thank you sailor," Boyle replied, "but I need to see your captain first. If that is possible."

"Certainly sir, I'll take you there first. If you and your crew would follow me, sir," he said, motioning, to the sedan.

Picking up their suitcases, the three men headed toward the car. The driver opened the trunk and then went to open the doors for the officers. Sparks put the suitcases in the trunk, closed it, and climbed in the back seat with Johnston.

Pulling away from the airplane, the navy blue sedan drove around the hangar on its way to the "Ready Room". Parking at the curb, the driver got out and opened Boyle's door for him. Boyle stepped out of the car, turned to the driver and said, "Why don't you take these two to their quarters and come back for me in about half an hour? I have some paperwork to take care of."

"Yes sir, that will be fine, sir."

Closing the door, the driver saluted Boyle once again. After the officer had returned his salute, he went around the car and slid behind the wheel. Boyle leaned in through the open window to speak to Johnston.

"Jim, when you get settled in, see if you can pick up a paper. When I get done with this FAA report, we'll go looking for a place."

"Sure thing, skipper," Johnston nodded, smiling. "See you in half an hour then?"

"Thirty minutes, buddy." Boyle touched the brim of his cap, turned and started toward the building.

As Boyle sauntered into the ready room, the sedan pulled away from the curb.

Boyle walked directly to the Squadron Commander's office. Pausing at the door, he took a deep breath and gathered his nerve for the tense confrontation that was about to take place.

Opening the door, Boyle stepped into the commander's outer office. It looked much the same as every other reception area he had been in. Maps on the walls, high backed recliner-type chairs, and gray filing cabinets crowned with stacks of paper. There was a coffeepot on a table in the corner; on the wall beside it hung the personalized mugs of each of the squadron's officers.

Boyle knocked on the captain's inner office door. When the captain called for him to enter he turned the doorknob and went in.

"Commander Charles Boyle reporting sir," he said stiffly.

"Good morning, Commander, welcome to NAS North Island," the captain said, rising to his feet to greet him, "stand easy commander. What can I do for you?"

Captain Wilson was a tall man, about six feet four inches, slender and fit. He had curly hair and a slight touch of gray around his ears. A thin, black mustache accented his rugged face. Boyle estimated the captain was about forty-five years old. Wilson's pale blue eyes were cold and piercing. There were harsh lines around his mouth. All at once, Boyle felt even more uneasy standing before him.

"Well, sir, we had a slight mishap on the way out here and I need to make out an incident report for the FAA"

Wilson chuckled quietly, "Yes, I've been expecting you. What happened up there to cause it? Someone accidentally turn on one of your jammers?"

Tensing uneasily, Boyle shifted his stance slightly and replied, "Yes sir, unfortunately that is exactly what happened."

A smile tugged at the corners of Wilson's mouth, "Please, Commander, call me Joe, and relax! I'm not going to bite your head off."

"Yes sir, Captain...I mean Joe. You can call me Charlie if you'd like."

Wilson nodded sympathetically; about as loose-limbed as a tiger at rest, "Certainly, Charlie. Now tell me what happened."

"Well Joe, I'm a bit embarrassed by the whole incident. I'm the one who did it. I went back to the radio compartment to stretch out and catch a short snooze. These cross-country flights can be tough; especially when you do them as infrequently as I do. Anyway, I bumped one of the power switches on my helmet unaware."

"Well Charlie, I should be quite upset about it but, confidentially, the same thing happened to me two years ago. One of my other pilots did it about two months ago too."

"Really, Joe?"

"Yeah, those darned switches are really in a bad place. I submitted a recommendation, for some kind of guards to be installed to protect against this sort of thing, about a year ago but, you know how slow the Pentagon can be."

Boyle nodded in agreement. He was relieved that Wilson had not flown off the handle, as his own captain would have.

"I'm not going to reprimand you for this incident, Charlie. I do hope, however, that you learned not to sleep on a cross-country flight."

"Thanks, Joe, I have."

"Good. Now then, you had better get those reports made out for the FAA; they have to be done in triplicate."

"I'd like to say thanks for being so understanding about this, Joe. I've been a nervous wreck, knowing I'd have to face you with this."

"With good reason, Charlie, but I'm not the one you need to be concerned with. The FAA can be pretty nasty about it if they want to."

"What did they do when it happened to you, sir?"

"Well, they fired a nasty letter off to the Pentagon and demanded that I be reprimanded. They wanted me grounded for a month or two and to undergo a reevaluation to see if I was mentally and physically fit to fly. The Pentagon didn't do it all, though, which was fortunate for me. I just ended up with a letter in my file."

"Good grief! That's all I need right now is another letter of reprimand."

"Yes, I heard about the other one," Wilson said, half smiling. "Did you really bomb the Kennedy with a bunch of flour sacks?"

"It was only two flour sacks, Joe. It was supposed to be a joke; my co-pilot had a bet with one of the guys aboard that we'd never be able to get close to the ship without being spotted. His was one of the planes that we hit."

"Well, Charlie, that wasn't very good judgment on your part."

"I know, Joe.

Wilson handed Boyle the form for his report. It was the standard multi-layered type with carbons between each sheet.

"Care for some coffee, Charlie?"

"Yes, Joe thanks."

Wilson took two of the mugs from their hooks. Handing one of them to Boyle, he turned and placed the other under the spout of the coffee maker.

Wilson stepped back, allowing Boyle to fill his.

"You can use the outer office to work on that report. There's a typewriter on the desk," he said, pointing to the large steel desk in the opposite corner.

"Thanks Joe."

Just then, the duty driver entered the room.

"You're crewmen are both over at the Officer's Quarters, sir. I'll be right down the hall whenever you are ready to go, sir."

"Thank you, Airman," Boyle replied.

The young man turned and started toward the door. He paused about half way through the doorway, turned and spoke once more.

"Ah…excuse me, sir, but I was wondering, if I might ask a favor, sir?"

"Sure, Airman; ask away."

"Well, sir, I don't mean to bother you…I know you're real busy and all but, I was wondering if you might have an empty seat for the flight back east. I haven't been home to see my folks in nigh onto a year and a half now. I've been waiting—for a hop going that away, sir."

"Sure thing, Airman, but you'll have to get it approved by Captain Wilson and get some leave papers made out in case of emergency."

"Yes, sir," he replied excitedly, "I've already done that…just in case you said yes, sir."

"That's what I call preparedness," Boyle chuckled.

The young man embarrassed by Boyle's response, nervously turned to leave.

"I'll leave you to your paperwork, sir. I'll be next door when you need me."

Boyle turned to his paperwork. He placed the papers into an old Smith-Corona typewriter that was on the desk. It took him almost twenty minutes to hunt-and-peck his way through the report but, at last, he finished.

Removing the papers from the machine, he rose to his feet, turned, and walked into Wilson's office, tapping on the door as he entered.

"Joe, I've finished the report. Would you like to look it over before I turn it in?"

"Yeah, Charlie; you can leave it here. I'll look it over and then forward it for you so that you can get out and do what you came here to do."

"Thanks, Joe. I'll need your driver for a couple of hours if that's okay?"

"Sure, Charlie; he's all yours," Wilson said, taking the report from Boyle. "Blake's a good kid. Wish I had more like him in this outfit."

Boyle left the office and found Blake.

"Ready to go, Blake," Boyle asked.

"Yes, sir," the young man replied.

The two men walked briskly to the navy blue sedan and got in.

"Did you say that both of my men are staying in the Officer's Quarters, Blake?"

"Yes sir, I did. There wasn't room in any of the enlisted men's barracks on base, so Captain Wilson made arrangements for him to stay there with you, sir."

"Good," Boyle replied, "That makes it simpler when we're ready to go." They pulled up in front of the white clapboard barracks that was reserved for visiting officers. It was a nice one-story building with a door at each end and windows down the two sides.

Once the car stopped, Blake jumped out and ran around to the other side to open the door for Boyle.

"Do me a favor, Blake, will you, please," Boyle said, stepping out of the car.

"Sure thing Commander, sir."

"Don't jump out to open my door like that; it embarrasses the heck out of me when you do."

"If that's what you want sir, okay, but I was told that it is my job as the duty driver to open doors for officers, sir."

"Well, I'll tell you what then, Blake, when we're on the base you can open it but as soon as we get off base you can relax, alright?"

"Yes sir, thank you."

Boyle walked into the barracks and found Johnston and Sparks.

"Did you get a paper, Jim?"

"Yes I did, skipper, but I'll tell you one thing; it's going to cost a lot more to live off-base here than it does out east."

"How much more?"

"About twice as much as it would cost in Virginia for a small apartment and even more for a house."

"Well, if we asked Sparks to go in with us, the three of us could afford a small house. What do you think of that, Sparks?"

"I was thinking of asking you that, skipper. Otherwise I'll have to live on base and rent a garage to keep the model in.

"Fine then; it's settled we'll go in together and rent a house with a garage. Right now, though, I want to take a shower. Then we can do some house shopping."

"Right, skipper, I'll look for something in the paper to use as a starting point," Johnston said.

Boyle went off to the shower. Johnston and Sparks each took a portion of the real estate ads and scanned them for suitable houses. By the time Boyle had gotten out of the shower, shaved, and dressed, the two men had found several addresses for them to look at.

"Blake," Johnston began, "do you know where any of these places are?" "Yes sir, most of them aren't very far from the base. This one's in a bad area though," he said, pointing to one of the ads.

"'Why don't we start with the closest one then," Sparks asked.

The men walked out to the navy blue sedan. Blake opened the doors for the officers to get in and went around to the other side. As they drove toward the gate, Boyle turned to Johnston and spoke.

"I told Blake not to bother with the doors like that when we get off base, Jim. I feel very self-conscious when he does it."

"I agree skipper," Johnston replied.

"I figured that you would, Jim"

They quickly arrived at the first address that was on the list. It was a quaint little three-bedroom bungalow. It had a screened-in porch across the front of it and an adequate two-car garage in the back. Best of all, it was within their price range. The landlord showed them around and the three men decided to take it. Together, they had enough cash to give the landlord the first and last month's rent as a security deposit.

"We'll be moving in next week," Boyle told him.

"That'll be fine, gentlemen; I'll keep an eye on the place until you do." Boyle and the others got back into the car and drove away.

"Where might we find a good place to eat that is not too expensive," Johnston asked.

"There are a couple of nice places about three miles down this road. Their prices are reasonable and the food is good. If you want fast food, there's a McDonald's about a half of a mile away on the next street over."

The three men decided on McDonald's. Blake turned the car and headed for the restaurant.

After lunch, the three men wanted to do some sightseeing. They decided not to use the Navy car; so they went back to a small place that they had passed on the way to the house. It was a motorcycle rental garage. There, each of them rented a motorcycle.

"Blake, you can go back to the base now. If we need you later, I'll call Captain Wilson. Otherwise, as far as I'm concerned, you can go back and pack for the trip tomorrow.

"Yes sir, Commander, thank you, sir. I'll see you tomorrow then, if not tonight," he said, returning to the car.

Blake drove off toward the naval base and the three men rode away in the other direction. They rode around the city looking for places that they would likely visit later. They found several bars, some grocery stores, a couple of movie theaters, and a hobby shop.

Sparks wanted to stop at the hobby shop to check the prices of some things that he needed for the model.

"I can meet you back at the motorcycle shop in about an hour, skipper" he offered.

"We can wait here, Sparks I doubt if it'll take you that long and besides we don't have anyplace that we have to be," Boyle responded.

Sparks went into the store. He walked out of the store about ten minutes later carrying a small brown paper bag.

"They have just about anything you could possibly want in there," he said excitedly, "I've been looking all over for these decals and haven't seen them anywhere back East."

The three men rode around for another hour, returned the motorcycles to the rental garage, and walked back to the base for diner.

Upon returning to the base, Boyle was handed a message to call Captain Wilson.

While Boyle made his call, the other two men changed clothes for diner. Boyle soon joined them and the trio left to go to the Officer's Mess to eat.

After diner, the three men had a few drinks at the Officer's Club and returned to their quarters for the night. The next day's flight back to Virginia was going to start very early.

CHAPTER FIVE

Dawn came early for the crew of Alpha-Papa-Seven-Three-Zero. This flight back to the east coast to pack up their belongings only to fly right back out to the west coast made it seem twice as bad.

It was five o'clock in the morning when Commander Boyle got out to the airplane to begin his pre-flight inspection. Airman Blake was already there, waiting. His bags were packed and sitting nearby. As the commander approached, the young airman came to attention and saluted the officer.

"Good morning, sir, I trust you slept well," he said with a very bright smile.

"Good morning, Blake. Thank you, yes I did sleep well."

"Is there anything that I can do to help get ready to go, commander?"

"No, Blake, thank you. Sparks and Lieutenant Commander Johnston will be here momentarily, and we'll be taking off as soon as they run through their checklists. Just sit tight, I know that you are anxious to get home for a couple of days. Don't worry; you'll be there in a few hours."

Boyle continued to walk around the plane. He checked the landing gear and the wings, the brake hoses and the engines, looking for any sign of wear or anything that could cause problems once they were in the air.

Sparks and Jim Johnston came walking up to the plane from the hangar. "Good morning, skipper, Blake," Sparks said with a half smile on his face.

"What are you grinning about, Sparks," questioned the commander.

"Oh, just happy to be alive and heading back east, skipper," he said very unconvincingly.

"Right, Sparks, and cows have wings too," retorted the commander briskly. "Come on, Sparks, out with it."

"Lieutenant Commander Johnston was just telling me about another one of his dreams, that's all, skipper," Sparks finally admitted.

"Oh, really; all right, Jim, what was this one about?"

"Awe, skipper, you don't really want to hear about it."

"Come on, spill it. If it's that good I want to hear it. I could use a good laugh at this hour of the morning."

"Well this one was really far out, even for me," he began, "you see, Sparks was standing by a car, parked on a runway. He was holding a television remote control transmitter. The car was loaded with C4, and he sent it speeding into the side of a busy airport terminal and detonated it."

"Good grief, Jim. What the devil were you drinking last night, torpedo juice?"

"That's just the point, skipper. I didn't even have a drink last night."

"Jim, I think you'd better see a doctor or someone about these dreams of yours. They seem to be getting worse," the commander replied with a very serious look on his face.

Boyle turned and went into the plane, followed closely by Sparks, Johnston, and Blake.

"Sparks, show Blake where to stow his gear and help him get strapped and plugged in, please," the pilot said.

"Aye, aye, skipper," Sparks replied.

Sparks opened a small compartment and told Blake to stow his gear in it and then pointed to the seat across the companionway from his own.

"You'll sit there, Blake. Your radio cord plugs into the small jack and your oxygen hose goes into the bigger one," he said pointing to the panel next to the seat. "This is your parachute harness and here is the lever for the ejection seat, just in case of trouble."

"Thanks, Sparks," Blake replied. "I know about the ejection system, I'm being trained as an ejection seat repairman."

"Ever flown in an A-3 before, Blake?"

"No, I haven't, Sparks. I have gone through flight crew survival training though. That is the only way they would let me fly back with you."

"Well, that is always a good idea whenever flying military anyway,"

Sparks replied, fastening his own seat belt and turning to his equipment.

Sparks went about flipping switches and turning dials, getting the radios warmed up and operational. Blake just sat and watched as Sparks went through his pre-flight checklist.

Sparks pressed the button for the intercom.

"Skipper," he said, "we're all set back here. I've set the assigned frequencies for today; any changes since last night?"

"No changes, Sparks. Is Blake all set?"

"Roger that, skipper, he's all strapped in and briefed."

"Well done, we'll be ready to go in about five minutes."

The two officers had almost completed their checklists when the ground crewman assigned to them came out of the hangar and plugged his headset into the plane's external intercom jack on the underside of the plane's nose.

"Commander Boyle, sir, this is Aviation Mechanic Third Class Jones. Good morning, sir," his voice crackled over the intercom. "I'm your ground crew for this morning. How are you coming along, sir?"

"Good morning, Jones. We are just about ready to startup," the pilot said. "Very well, sir; request permission to connect the starting unit."

"Permission granted, Jones, we can finish up the last few items once we are started."

"Aye, aye, sir."

Once the cable from the starting unit was plugged in, Jones stepped back so that the pilot could see him clearly and gave him the hand signal to start his port side engine. Boyle flipped the switches pressed the button to start the engine. The turbine blades began to turn and the engine caught. Once it was running, Jones gave the signal to start the starboard side engine. When both engines were running and the gauges were registering proper operation, Boyle signaled Jones to remove the power cable.

Jones disconnected the cable and moved the starting unit out of the way. Then he waited for Boyle to signal that all was in order and that he was ready to taxi out.

Boyle gave a "thumbs-up", signaling that all was in order. Then he signaled the ground crewman to remove the wheel chocks. Jones ducked under the wing and removed the wooden wheel blocks. Then he moved off to the side, signaled Boyle to turn his nose wheel to the left and release his brakes. The A3 started to roll forward and to the left. As the plane came around and was facing the main taxiway, Jones saluted the pilot.

Commander Boyle returned his salute and pushed the throttle levers forward slightly. The second transcontinental flight of Alpha-Papa-Seven-Three-Zero was under way.

"North Island Tower, this is Alpha-Papa-Seven-Three-Zero. Communications check, over."

"We read you Lima-Charlie, Seven-Three-Zero, over."

"North Island; request take-off clearance and last minute instructions, over."

"Seven-Three-Zero, you are cleared for take-off on runway three-right. There is a storm over Denver at about twenty-five thousand, over."

"Roger North Island, thanks a lot. We'll be seeing you in a few days, out."

Boyle taxied to the end of the assigned runway and stopped. He pushed the throttle controls forward and released the brakes. The A3 lurched forward and began to pick up speed as it headed down the runway; within minutes Alpha-Papa-Seven-Three-Zero had climbed through a thin layer of wispy clouds and leveled off at thirty-three thousand feet heading due east with airspeed of six hundred and thirty-two miles per hour.

"Smoke them if you want them, gentlemen," Boyle said over the intercom. "I'm going to autopilot now. We'll be in Virginia in about six hours or less, depending on that storm over Denver."

None of the three crew members felt much like talking about the trip back, and both Sparks and Johnston were afraid to speak about the dreams in front of Blake, after all he had heard too much already. It was pretty quiet in the plane for most of the trip.

The storm that they had been warned about, over Denver, was far enough below them that the crew and passenger of Alpha-Papa-Seven-Three-Zero had a very uneventful trip back to the ease coast.

"Well, men, we're almost home, or should I say we're almost there."

"Skipper, how long do you figure we have until we have to leave to go back to California?" Sparks asked.

"Well, the captain said a week, so I guess about four more days, Sparks," the commander replied. "Why?"

"Well, I have to figure how to pack the model in such a way that nothing gets damaged, and I have to do something with my car and the house."

"You can sub-let the house, can't you?" Johnston asked.

"I don't see any reason why the Navy wouldn't let you take your car with you," was the commander's reply.

"That would just leave the house. If I sub-let it out with the understanding that when Bill gets back from sea he has a place to stay and that the lease is only until I get back from California, I suppose that would work."

"Just make sure that all of that is in writing, Sparks," Boyle continued. "I'm sure that you won't have any trouble getting someone in time to be ready. If you don't, I imagine you can find a Realtor or someone you can trust to handle it for you."

By this time it was time for them to prepare for landing. Boyle radioed the tower for landing instructions, while Johnston went through the landing checklist. Once this was completed, Boyle put the plane into position for landing. The landing was smooth and easy. They taxied up to the hangar and shut everything off.

Blake was excited to finally arrive in Virginia. He, unlike the others on board, was glad to be there, even if only for a few days.

"Well, Blake, here you are, at home. I told you that I'd get you here safe and sound," the pilot said with a smile.

"That you did, sir, that you did, and I'm very grateful. With your permission, sir, I'd like to leave right away so that I can go and surprise my girl. I didn't tell her that I was coming home today."

"Sure, Blake, where does she live? Maybe one of us will be going that way and could give you a ride."

"I live on the next street over, skipper. I'll be glad to give him a ride just as soon as we're done here," Sparks offered.

"Great, why don't the two of you go ahead and take off then. Jim and I can finish up here and then we'll be taking off too."

"Okay, skipper, thanks. By the way, if you'd like to fly the model again before we go, it will have to be today or tomorrow. I'll have to start packing it up after that."

"Yeah, Sparks. I'd like to take another turn or two with it, if you don't mind; how about tomorrow morning?"

"Sure, skipper, I'll be ready about six. We can leave for the field as soon as you arrive. I'll have everything loaded and ready to go."

"Okay, Sparks. See you in the morning then."

Sparks and Blake took their bags and headed for Sparks' car. When they had gotten into the car, Blake asked about the model.

"What kind of plane is it that you have?"

"It is a scale model Boeing 747."

"Oh, really; how big is it?"

"Well, it has an eight foot wing span, and it is nine and a half feet long. The tip of the vertical stabilizer is two and a half feet off of the ground. It's one twenty-fourth of the actual size, and it is radio controlled."

"Wow that sure must be some fun to fly!" Blake exclaimed.

"I don't know about that, I can't fly it, but it sure is exciting to watch Commander Boyle do it."

By this time Sparks had driven out the main gate of the base and was heading for home. Blake asked if he could see the model before going to his girlfriend's house.

"I can walk over from your place. I fly model planes myself and yours sounds fascinating."

Sparks agreed and soon the two men arrived at his home.

When Sparks opened the garage door and removed the sheet that was covering the model, Blake could hardly believe his eyes. The sight of the model was beyond words. The attention to detail, as well as the sheer size, really astounded him.

"Man, are you bringing this thing to California, Sparks," he asked.

"Sure am. I have to crate it up tomorrow after we take it out for a flight in the morning."

Blake was very excited. He told Sparks how he had started a model airplane flying club in San Diego two years before. The biggest plane in the club was also a hand made plane, a model of a B-17 bomber, but it was nothing compared to this one. Blake asked Sparks if he'd mind an extra person on hand at the following morning's test flight. Sparks replied that it would be fine with him and told him where they were going to be. He also told him that they would arrive at about six thirty or a few minutes earlier. Blake thanked him for showing him the model and then left for his girlfriend's house on the next block.

Sparks put his suitcase in the house and then went back out to the garage to prepare the model for the next day's activities.

Once the model was loaded onto the trailer and strapped down securely, Sparks closed and locked the garage and got into his car to leave.

Sparks drove over to the same bar in which he and the two officers had been drinking a couple of nights before.

Although he had not planned on seeing the two officers that night, Sparks met up with them when he walked into the bar.

"Well, well, Jim. Look who's here," Charlie Boyle said waving to Sparks to join them.

"Listen Sparks," the commander began, "as long as we're all going to be living in the same house, when we aren't on the base or around other military people, you can call me Charlie. Okay?"

"Sure, Charlie," he replied.

"That goes for me too, Sparks. My name is Jim, not Lieutenant Commander Johnston."

"I'11 drink to that, Jim," the commander said, raising his glass into the air. "All of this formality really bugs me after a while." The three men sat and talked for awhile and then left to go home for the night.

The next day dawned bright and clear, and by seven o'clock all four of the men were out at the old airport getting the model ready for take-off.

The second flight of Alpha-Papa-Seven-Three-Zero-Junior was about to begin.

"Sparks," Charlie Boyle asked, "how much of a fuel capacity do you have in this thing?"

"Well skipper, there are two five gallon tanks; one in each wing, and a two gallon tank in the fuselage."

"How much time does that give us?"

"The engines burn a gallon of fuel in just a little over a minute, when running at full throttle. That gives you about ten to twelve minutes of actual flying time at less than full throttle, allowing for take-off and landing time."

"Good then, how about if we see just how long she will go with about half throttle?"

Charlie Boyle pressed the buttons and started the four jet engines. Then he taxied the plane to the end of the runway and applied the brakes. Pushing the throttle controls only half way forward he released the brakes. The big model lurched forward and began to pick up speed. Soon the big model was airborne.

Charlie Boyle called Sparks over to take control of the plane.

"Here Sparks, it's your plane, fly it," he said smiling brightly. Sparks took the control box and began steering the plane in a gradual circle. Suddenly the model went into a sharp climb. The engines were straining to keep enough thrust coming to accommodate the speed requirements for such a climb.

Boyle rushed over and took the controls from Sparks just as the plane began to stall and plunge nose first towards the ground. Skillfully and masterfully the commander regained control of the plane and got it to fly level once again.

"Skipper, you just saved me a bunch of money and work," Sparks said, obviously shaken by the near accident.

"Don't worry, Sparks, all it takes is a little practice and you'll get the hang of it."

"Sure skipper, if I don't destroy it first."

Sparks walked off to the side to watch as Jim Johnston went to the commander for his chance to try the controls.

Jim took control of the plane and began to fly it in a tight circle. Suddenly, one of the engines began to make a coughing sound and then it just quit.

"Sounds like you're out of gas, Jim," Charlie Boyle said.

"We shouldn't be out yet," he said, "there must be something else wrong. There should be at least two more minutes left before it runs out. I'll bring it in anyway, though."

Jim brought the plane around into the wind. He pressed the button to lower the landing gear. All four bogies came down and locked into position. Jim pressed the control for the flaps to come down and for the air brakes to go on. The plane quickly slowed down and came in for the landing. It was a picture perfect landing and Jim was beaming with pride. He was smiling from ear to ear as he taxied the big model over to Sparks, who was waiting to find out why the engine had stopped.

"Looks like a blocked fuel filter to the number three engine, Lieutenant Commander," Sparks reported. "You did a great job of bringing her in, especially without an engine."

"I'd say the three of you have nothing to worry about when you go up in a real plane when you've got two pilots who can fly like that," Blake added.

"You've got that right, Blake," Sparks replied.

After a few adjustments, a new fuel filter, and topping off the fuel tanks, Sparks told the officers that the plane was ready for take-off. This time Blake had the privilege of piloting the model into the air. There he performed a few tricks with the plane. First, a slow barrel roll to the right followed by a lazy figure eight. The two officers were amazed at the young man's ability to handle the model, especially doing aerobatics.

"You handle the plane so naturally, Blake, have you been flying radio controlled planes for long," Boyle asked.

"Yes, sir; I've been flying them since I was twelve years old. I've always wanted to be a pilot, but my eyes aren't good enough to be a military pilot, so I just fly models."

Blake then put the model into a sharp climb. He took the plane up to about a hundred feet and then put it into a steep dive. At about forty feet he pulled back on the control stick and pushed it to the side to make the plane do an aileron roll. The three men stood and watched in amazement as Blake made the model do several more tricks before bringing it in for a landing to refuel.

When he had brought the plane in and taxied it over to Sparks, Blake said that he had to leave. He thanked Sparks for the chance to fly the 747.

"You've got one fantastic plane there, Sparks," he said, "if you'd like me to I'll gladly give you some flying lessons when we get back to California."

"I might just take you up on that, Blake."

Blake left, and Sparks refueled the model. This time Jim Johnston took the plane up and put it through its paces. Everything was going well until the plane suddenly turned and started flying off in a straight line away from the three men. It was headed toward the main road and away from the airport. Jim tried, unsuccessfully, several times to get it to turn back but there was no response. Sparks, realizing what was happening, quickly ran to his car and turned on his CB radio. Keying the microphone, he spoke sharply into it.

"Anyone on Old Mill Road, close to the old airport, who is using a citizens band radio, please stop transmission."

Sparks called for Jim to bring the control box and then he started the car. Both officers ran over to the car and jumped in. Sparks sped off in pursuit of the runaway airplane.

Sparks again keyed the microphone on the CB and repeated his plea for whoever was on the radio to stop transmitting. After briefly explaining what was happening and why he was asking them to stop transmitting, Sparks was at last able to overtake the runaway plane and Jim was able to regain control over it, turn it around, and fly it back to the airport.

"You see," Sparks began, "that guy was transmitting on the same frequency as the control box. His output power was strong enough to over ride our signal and he took the plane away just by keying his mike."

"That could really get to be a problem for someone if he were always being followed by model airplanes," Jim laughed.

"It could also get pretty expensive for the plane's owner if he wasn't able to catch up with it like we just did. Bill lost a couple that way. Never found a trace of them either," Sparks replied in a somber tone.

Once they were safely on the airport grounds and had the plane on the ground again, the three men agreed that they had had enough excitement for one day.

After the plane was dismantled and everything was strapped securely onto the trailer, the trio headed for Sparks' home. When they got there the two officers helped Sparks unload the plane and create it and the trailer up in preparation for the trip to California.

CHAPTER SIX

Moving day arrived all too quickly. Sparks had gotten the model and the trailer safely packed up and had taken all of his personal belongings and clothing that he could and packed them in his car. The Navy had agreed to move all of their belongings to California, including their cars. Sparks had found another sailor in his squadron who agreed to the terms of the sub-lease on the house and had moved in the day before. The squadron commander had assigned a couple of men to each of the three crewmen to help them get their things to the squadron's hangar to be picked up by a cargo plane the day after they were due to leave. The men took a truck to Sparks' home to pick up a couple of items of furniture, the crated model, and the trailer. Sparks drove his car to the airbase.

Sparks, Commander Boyle, and Lieutenant Commander Johnston went to see their commanding officer, who wished them well and then sent them on their way. He assured them that their belongings would be along the next day.

The crew of Alpha-Papa-Seven-Three-Zero met up with their passenger, Airman Blake, when they went out to their plane. Their third transcontinental flight, in a week's time, was about to begin.

The flight back to the West Coast was very long and tiring for the three men. It was also uneventful. The jet lag that many world travelers talk about was starting to become real, even to Commander Boyle. Even Blake had very little to say. His trip home had been very nice; he had totally surprised his girlfriend.

They had had a wonderful time together, but it just wasn't long enough.

By the time Commander Boyle landed the plane in California, both he and his crew were ready for a good night's sleep.

But, sleep was not in the Navy's plan for this trio.

Immediately upon their arrival to the new squadron, things began to change. The captain, who had been so nice and accommodating on their first trip out, suddenly became a tyrant. There was no time to rest; the training must start immediately. Commander Boyle and his men were told that they had been scheduled to start their first class as soon as they arrived. Much to his dismay, Commander Boyle's argument of being too tired fell upon deaf ears.

The captain assigned three of his radio operators to Sparks and instructed them to go with him to the Ready Room for a class on jamming techniques.

By the time Commander Boyle and Lieutenant Commander Johnston finished with their classes it was time for dinner. Sparks had finished about thirty minutes earlier and had caught a ride out to the house that they had rented. He was waiting on the front lawn when the two officers arrived.

"Sparks, glad to see you were able to get out of there," Charlie Boyle said walking up the driveway.

"Well, I'm not, skipper. I was, until I got here and found people in the house that we rented last week."

"What?" Boyle exclaimed.

"That's right, skipper," he continued, "It seems that the landlord that we talked to, and gave our money to last week is a con artist. It looks like we've been scammed. I called the police and they told me that we are the third ones this week who have reported this happening, all at this same address alone."

Boyle and Johnston both cursed and swore that they'd kill the guy who had done this to them if they ever caught up with him.

"Now what do we do, skipper?" Jim asked.

"Well, I for one do not intend to step foot on that base tonight. I'm getting a hotel room."

"I'm with you there, skipper. If we went back on base they'd probably put us to work again," Johnston said only half jokingly.

The three men headed for a nearby hotel and checked in for the night. Boyle called Captain Wilson and asked him if he could do anything to help them find a place to stay since most of their money had been given to the phony landlord.

Captain Wilson said that he would make arrangements for the officers to stay in the base's officer's quarters and that Sparks could stay in the enlisted men's barracks.

The three, very disgusted, men went out and got drunk in one of the nearby bars that night.

The next day, Charlie and Jim moved into the BOQ. Sparks moved into the enlisted barracks. Then the day's work began. Sparks set up a jammer on the bench in the avionics shop. He took it apart, piece by piece, and explained what each piece was for, how it worked, and what to do if it failed. It made for a very long and tedious day.

By four o'clock, sixteen hundred hours, that afternoon, all three men were ready to head out to look for another house to rent. All three had had very difficult times during the day and were thoroughly fed up. Commander Boyle borrowed a Navy car from the base motor pool, and they drove toward the main gate to leave the base.

Upon their arrival at the front gate, they were stopped and the guard handed Boyle a note. It read *"Urgent! Contact Captain Wilson immediately!"*

"You can use the phone in my guard shack, sir," the sentry told him. "I'll have to ask you to have one of your men park the car off to the side though, sir."

Sparks got behind the wheel and drove the black sedan to the designated parking area and turned off the key to wait for Commander Boyle to return.

It wasn't long before Boyle returned. He was madder than either of the two men had ever seen him be, in all of the time they had been together.

"What's wrong, Charlie?" Jim asked.

"I just spoke to Captain Wilson," he began, "the Air Force C-141 cargo plane that was carrying our cars and belongings out here from Virginia crashed and exploded on take-off, killing everyone on board, and destroying all of our belongings."

"No," Sparks shouted, in shock and disbelief, "not my model! Please, tell me that my model wasn't destroyed."

"Yes, Sparks; your model, your car, my car, Jim's car; everything is gone."

Sparks swore loudly and slammed his fist down on the trunk of the car. His actions caught the attention of the sentry but Boyle assured him that everything was all right.

"Four years of sweat, two thousand dollars, all gone. All because of this idiotic assignment! Why do they feel like they have to screw with our lives like this? "

"I understand how you feel, Sparks. Believe me, I do," was all his commander could manage to say by way of consolation.

"That settles it for me," Jim Johnston yelled, "I'm going to resign my commission and get out of here right now. How much are we supposed to sacrifice for this country?"

"Now, Jim," Boyle said, "you don't want to go and do that, not really. I know you just got gut-kicked and you have a right to be mad as a wet hen right now, but just hold on. Everything is insured. We'll get paid for all of it. Somehow, someway, we'll see some sort of justice for all of the aggravation but we just have to keep our wits about us."

"That's not the point, Charlie," Jim started, "they come along, disrupt our lives, lie to us, some asshole robs us, and now this! What's next?"

"I don't know, Jim, but look at it this way. It can't get much worse, can it?"

"Skipper, I'd like to request emergency leave to go back there to see if there is anything left of my plane," Sparks said, almost pleading.

"It's fine with me, Sparks, but you'll have to clear it with Captain Wilson. We're in his ballpark now and have to go by his rules."

"Okay, skipper, I'll go see him first thing in the morning."

"Better let me do it, Sparks. I might be able to talk him into letting you go and not charging it against your leave time."

"Thanks, Skipper, I really appreciate that."

The three men drove back to their respective barracks and slept there that night.

In the morning, Commander Boyle went to see Captain Wilson. He explained the situation surrounding Sparks' unique problem and his subsequent request. Wilson granted Sparks one week to go back to try to salvage his equipment from the plane's wreckage. He said that he would try to find Sparks a military hop to save him the airfare.

The next day, Sparks was on his way back to Virginia, this time by commercial air. There weren't any military flights going east for several days and Sparks didn't want to wait.

Sparks picked up his ticket at the airline ticket counter in the San Diego airport and checked all of his worldly possessions; one duffel bag. It felt really strange to be checking in and getting onto a real 747 to go back east; especially after having made the same trip several times during the past couple of weeks in an A-3. Sparks went out and got right on board the 747. It was a big plane, seats for five hundred people, six galleys, sixteen restrooms, and the spiral staircase that went up to the penthouse seats behind the cockpit. It was amazing to be in a real 747 after all of this time. He had worked on the model using sketches that Bill made, and books from the library.

Sparks went and sat down in one of the coach seats, near a window. The plane quickly filled up with people, most of them going to New York, but a few, like Sparks, were going to Virginia from there.

The 747 took off on time, which really surprised some of the people. When they had gotten up to they're cruising altitude, forty-three thousand feet, the pilot made the announcement over the intercom that people could smoke if they liked. He also gave a brief explanation of the plane's escape hatches and oxygen supplies.

Sparks got up from his seat and went over to one of the bars that were in the airplane. He ordered a bourbon and water. When his drink came; he asked the stewardess if passengers were ever allowed in the cockpit.

The stewardess said no; passengers were not allowed to just go up to the cockpit. They had to be invited by the pilot, but that rarely happened. Sparks finished his drink and ordered another.

Then he told the stewardess about the model and his reason for flying back to Virginia. She said that she would talk to the pilot and see what could be done. Sparks thanked her and went back to his seat.

It was almost a half-hour after his conversation at the bar that the stewardess came over to his seat.

"Mr. Greene, the captain has asked me to escort you up to the lounge in the penthouse to meet him."

"Why thank you ma'am," he replied.

Sparks got out of his seat and followed the stewardess up the spiral staircase and into the lounge. The stewardess led him over to a tall, dark man with a receding hairline and introduced him to the pilot.

"Captain Blaire, this is the young man that I was telling you about, Mr. Greene. Mr. Greene, this is our pilot, Captain Blaire."

"Jenny tells me that you've built a working, scale model of one of these babies, Mr. Greene."

"Yes, Captain, I have. Please, though, call me Sparks. All of my friends call me Sparks."

"Okay Sparks, but tell me, why do they call you Sparks? Is it because of the model?"

"No, it's because I'm a radio and radar repairman in the Navy."

"Oh, I see. You're a handy person to have around in the air. So tell me about your model, Sparks. How big is it?"

"It was, just a little over nine feet long, with a wing span of eight feet." "Was?"

"Yes, an Air Force C-141 cargo plane was transporting it, out to the West Coast, California, the other day. The cargo plane crashed on take-off and exploded, destroying it and everything else that it was carrying. I'm going back to see if there is anything salvageable."

"That's really a shame, Sparks; I hope you can save at least some of it."

"Yes, so do I. I really had a lot of time and money invested in it."

"Tell you what, why don't you join me and come up to the cockpit, and have a look around?"

"I was hoping to do exactly that, Captain. As I was telling the stewardess, this is the first time I've ever been in one of these things. All I've ever had to work with were pictures and books."

The pilot led the way and took Sparks up to the cockpit to look around. He introduced him to the co-pilot and the navigator, the radio operator was busy so he didn't interrupt.

"We're flying on the auto-pilot right now," he said, "ordinarily, on these cross-country flights; we simply put the plane on auto and let it go. Either the co-pilot or I will sit there and keep an eye on things, just in case of trouble, but George does the work. That gives us a little bit of a break from sitting all of the time."

"Yes, I know what that is like. My skipper, copilot, and I have had to fly across country three times this last week alone. It's really a drag,"

"You can certainly say that again," said the navigator.

"Well, Captain, I want to thank you for letting me come up here, I'11 get out of your way now. I really appreciate your taking the time to see me."

"You're very welcome, Sparks. Thank you for flying with us."

Sparks left the cockpit, found his way back down the spiral staircase, and over to his own seat, where he tried in vain to fall asleep, he was exhausted but also excited about having been allowed into the cockpit.

The weather wasn't very good outside, but in spite of that the landing at La Guardia was so smooth that if the stewardess hadn't awakened him to put on his seat belt, Sparks wouldn't have known that they had even landed. Sparks had to get off of the jumbo jet in New York and take a smaller plane to Virginia. There just weren't enough people going from California to Virginia to justify a jumbo jet going direct.

Sparks went to the baggage claim area to get his duffel bag. He had been told to pick it up, since there would be a three-hour layover between flights. The airlines didn't want to be responsible for baggage sitting for that long of a period of time.

When he got to the baggage claim area, it was a real madhouse. There were people everywhere, pushing and shoving; grabbing at anything that even looked similar to theirs. Sparks stood back until the crowd had thinned out a little before attempting to pick out his duffel bag. He made his way up to the conveyor belt and looked for his luggage. Finally he spied one that looked like his, but a tall thin man with blond hair picked it up and left. Two more pieces of the same size and shape started to come his way, but these too were snatched up and quickly disappeared into the crowd.

Soon, there was a lull in the amount of luggage coming in, but his was not there. A short time later, another batch of luggage started coming in and a new crowd of people started pushing and grabbing at the suitcases. It soon became evident to Sparks that his duffel bag had either been picked up by mistake by someone else or it was still on the plane.

Sparks, trying very hard to remain calm, walked over to a desk which had a sign that read "Lost and Found" and reported his luggage missing. A pretty red haired girl of about twenty-five was working at the desk. She took down the description of his duffel bag along with his name and address, his destination and flight number.

"I'm terribly sorry that this has happened, sir, I will try to locate it for you and get it to you in Virginia before you leave to go back to California."

Her pleasant attitude and pretty face had a calming effect on Sparks' own attitude at that particular moment. He felt like she was really sincere and would honestly make an effort to locate his duffel bag. He thanked her for her time and went on his way, confident that he would find his duffel bag either waiting for him in Virginia or else following closely behind him there.

The next leg of his journey was even more disquieting. The weather, all of the way down the East Coast, was terrible. Many of the airports had been closed and their inbound flights had to be diverted. The flight that Sparks was on was no different. The airport that he was supposed to go to had to close due to a very dense fog. Sparks and the rest of the passengers of his flight were told that they were going to try to land in Baltimore, and that bus transportation would be provided for them to go on to Virginia.

The landing was very bumpy and rough. The weather in Baltimore was not much better than what they were told it was like in Virginia. It was raining and very foggy. The bus to Virginia was an hour and a half late arriving at the airport, due to weather related accidents that were tying up the roads, Sparks finally arrived in Virginia, at three o'clock in the morning. Cold, wet, and tired, and without as much as a dry pair of socks, he was a very unhappy man. Sparks went to the house, where he had been living before going to California. There were no lights on in the house. There was no car in the garage, so Sparks took out his key to the garage and opened the door.

Figuring that he could sleep in the garage, out of the rain for a few hours, he sat down on a pile of newspapers and leaned his head against the wall and went to sleep.

About fifteen minutes had passed when a bright light was shining in his eyes and a rough voice telling him not to move quickly awakened Sparks. Sparks opened his eyes slowly, finding it hard to see with the beam of a policeman's flashlight shining directly in his face. He raised one arm to shield his face from the light, and found himself hurtling across the room.

Again the light was in his eyes, but this time he didn't move. "Whoever you are, please turn your light away from my face so that I can open my eyes," he said cautiously.

"This is the police. Don't move. Who are you and what are you doing in here?"

"My name is Joe Greene. I rent this house from Clarence Ford. I've sub-let it to a friend of mine, in my squadron, who isn't home right now, while I was in California. I've come back for a few days and needed a place to stay for the night. I have my I.D. card in my right hip pocket if you will let me I'll get it out and I'll show you."

"Okay, get up slowly. Keep your right hand in front of you and reach around with your left to get it out and don't try anything. "

Sparks held his right hand out in front of him and fumbled to reach his opposite pocket with his left hand. He finally got his wallet out of his pocket and opened it for the officer to see his I.D.

"Okay, Mr. Greene. You are who you say you are, but how do I know that what you are saying about being here is true?"

Sparks showed the officer his driver's license and car registration papers, both of which listed his address as that of the house in which they were standing.

"Okay, sir. I'm sorry about all of this, but the guy who was living here was killed in a plane crash a couple of days ago, and we've been told to watch the house."

"Was it the Air Force cargo plane that was going to California?"

"Yes, I think so. Why?"

"Because, everything that I owned was on that plane, and got destroyed. That's why I came back."

"Man, you really have had it rough, haven't you?"

"That's not even the half of it, officer."

"Well, I guess that I'll be moving on now, Mr. Greene. I'll alert headquarters so that no one will bother you anymore while you're here."

"Thank you officer," Sparks said, and then went into the house for the rest of the night.

CHAPTER SEVEN

The next morning Sparks got up, showered, shaved, and got dressed in some of the clothes that Bill had packed away in a closet. After breakfast, he went out to the garage and uncovered Bill's motorcycle, which had also been put away until his return from sea.

Sparks left the house and rode over to the base. He went down to the squadron's hangar and went in to see a couple of the guys in the radio shop. They told him about the crash and the fire that followed. They told him that Gerry, the guy who had rented his house, had been assigned to escort their belongings, as a security guard. Neither he nor any of their belongings had survived the crash.

Sparks went to see the captain. He needed permission to enter the crash sight to see if he could try to salvage anything from his model. The captain said that he did not have the authority to allow anyone to enter the area until the FAA and the Navy investigators had gone through it all. He told Sparks that he would call the FAA investigator and explain the situation and see if they would allow him to join in the search. The captain said that as soon as he heard from them, he would notify Sparks at home.

At about three-thirty in the afternoon the call came; Sparks had permission to join the FAA field team and look for his equipment, but he would not be allowed to remove anything from the crash site until it had been photographed and examined.

Sparks hurried out to the crash site. There was an area of grass about the size of two football fields that was scorched and blackened. There were pieces of the airplane and burnt out remains of the three cars, scattered over an area about three hundred yards in diameter. Considering the fact that the C-141 had been one hundred and sixty-eight feet long with a wingspan of one hundred and sixty feet with four giant turbine jet engines there were a great many pieces. The six bodies of the crew had been removed to the morgue as soon as they were found the day of the crash.

The devastation was worse than Sparks could have imagined. The men from the FAA and the Navy's people were combing the area with the utmost of care. Searching, very carefully, through the wreckage for a clue that would help them figure out why the plane had crashed. The pieces that they were finding were being carefully moved into a nearby hangar in an attempt to reconstruct as much of the plane and its load as possible, within a roped off area.

One of the men found the four small jet engines from Sparks' model. They were melted and badly deformed from the heat of the fire. There wasn't a trace of the rest of the model. The control box was also melted and useless; Sparks left the crash site a broken man. Not only had he lost a friend in that crash, but also he had lost everything else that he had owned.

Sparks caught a plane bound for New York and then another for the return to California. It had been a total waste of time and money to come back.

On the way back to California Sparks had a lot of time to think. He was troubled by some of the thoughts but considered them carefully, just the same.

When the plane landed in San Diego, Sparks remembered his duffel bag, which had gotten lost in New York. He had forgotten all about it and didn't even check on it when he had been there on the way back. Sparks went to the lost and found desk in the San Diego airport and told the girl there his story. She assured him that she would check with New York by Teletype, and try to locate his bag and then have it sent over to the base when it arrived.

Sparks left the airport by cab, and headed for the Naval Air Station. He was not at all happy to be back, as a matter of fact he was very unhappy, about everything. When the cab stopped at the front gate of the base, Sparks got out, paid the driver and then walked through the gate and went to his barracks.

Shortly after arriving back at the barracks, Sparks was told that he had a phone call. When he answered the phone he found that it was Charlie Boyle on the other end of the line.

"Hello Skipper, how are you," he said, trying to be cheerful.

"Fair, Sparks, fair. How about you, how are you doing? I heard about Gerry that's too bad. Was he a close friend?"

"No, he wasn't a close friend, but he was a friend just the same."

Sparks went on to relate some of his experiences during his trip, how his duffel bag had gotten lost, and the policeman had roughed him up in the garage. He told Charlie about the utter devastation of the plane and all of their belongings and how fed up and angry he was over the whole situation.

"Well sit tight kid, Jim and I will be right over to pick you up. We have some good news for you. Sounds like you could really use it about now. We'll be there in about five minutes."

The phone went dead at the other end as the commander hung up. Sparks wondered what could be such good news. Had they been transferred back to the East Coast already? Had the police caught the phony landlord and gotten the money that they had paid for rent back? What could be good news at this point in his life? These were the questions that Sparks asked himself as he waited for the two officers to arrive.

His answer came very soon; the two officers drove up in a nice, shiny new, red Camaro.

"Come on Sparks," Jim Johnston shouted, we've got something to show you."

Sparks ran out and got into the car. He was impressed but still not excited.

"We've got some good news for you, Sparks. The police haven't caught the guy who ripped us off, yet, but we've got a place to stay for as long as we need it," the commander said with a big smile.

"Oh yeah Skipper? Where is this place that it makes you look so happy?" "It is north of here a little ways. It's a beach house in LaJolla, just like the ones in the movies. But the best news is that we have it rent free."

"Rent free," Sparks exclaimed excitedly. "How in the world could we get a place rent free at the beach?"

"Jim's mother has a friend who is living back east for awhile, working on his Master's degree and he said that we could use it for as long as we want."

"Skipper, you've just made a very bad day a whole lot better. When do we move in?"

"We did, yesterday. All you have to do is get your stuff out of your locker and we'll head out there now."

"The three men got out of the car and went into the enlisted men's barracks where Sparks got his things out of his locker. There wasn't much to gather up, what hadn't been destroyed in the crash or gotten lost in his duffel bag didn't really amount to much. The three men went back outside and got into the car and headed toward the main gate.

"The insurance will cover your car and your clothes, as well as most of your investment in the model," Charlie Boyle told Sparks.

"Too bad it doesn't cover all of the time that Bill and I spent working on it," Sparks replied angrily.

"I know how you feel, kid. Try not to let it eat at you though," he recommended.

They drove on in silence, out onto the main highway that headed North. It was a beautiful day, the sun was warm and the sky was very blue.

It didn't take long for Sparks to begin to relax and enjoy the scenery.

Jim drove the car up the main highway, until they came to an exit, whose sign read "LaJolla", where he turned off. They drove for a short time on this road and then turned off, onto a small road that led to the beach, They pulled into the driveway of a nice looking, modern beach house that sat about a hundred yards back from the water's edge.

"Well, Sparks, this is it," Jim said with a gleam in his eye. "It's nice inside but, it's great outside," he said pointing to a group of very attractive young girls in bikinis.

"I get your meaning loud and clear, Jim. This could be a very interesting time after all," Sparks replied, his spirits beginning to lift. Sparks got his things out of the trunk, and the three men went inside.

Once he had unpacked his things and settled in, Sparks related the events of his trip east to the two officers, who listened intently.

"You know, Sparks, if that had happened to me, I don't know what I'd do. I really don't think that I would have been as calm as you were. I'd probably have slugged someone just to let off steam," Jim replied, when Sparks had finished.

"I'll tell you, Jim, if there was ever a time when I felt like going after an airline, that was definitely it," Sparks told him.

Jim and Charlie both nodded their heads in agreement; it had been a very frustrating time for their comrade.

Just then, the phone began to ring. The call was for Charlie Boyle.

"Who knows that we're here," Sparks queried.

"I left this number at the duty desk this morning. Just in case Old Slave-driver Wilson wanted to get a hold of us," the commander replied.

Charlie took the call, and from the look on his face during the conversation, he wasn't at all happy about it.

When he had hung up the phone Charlie went to his room and began changing into his flight suit and boots.

"What's up, skipper," Jim asked.

"I have to go up with another one of those training flights in forty-five minutes. Nobody knew how to get in touch with me to let me know about it until now though," he said, obviously annoyed by the interruption of his time off, "Do you want me to drive you in or what," Jim asked, "Yes, that way you guys can have the car. This flight is supposed to last until about ten o'clock tonight, so I'11 stay on base tonight and ride out with you tomorrow."

The two officers got into the car and started back towards the base. Sparks stayed behind and just relaxed for awhile.

When Jim returned from dropping off the commander, he and Sparks talked about some more of the strange dreams Jim had had the last few nights.

"I had a real gem the other night," Jim began. "Sparks, you won't believe this one. I dreamt that we pulled off the remote hijacking and picked up ten million dollars in ransom and got away, scot-free."

"Jim, have you ever thought about writing these dreams down; like in a notebook or something."

"No Sparks, why should I do that?"

"Well, just so that we could study them. The whole thing that you've laid out fascinates me. If you put them all together, maybe we could find out what you're thinking about that would cause them."

Jim agreed to begin writing down everything that he could remember about the dreams that he had had in the past, and that he would write down any future ones as soon after waking up as possible.

At about eleven thirty that night, both Sparks and Jim had the feeling that something was wrong with the commander's flight.

It was an unexplainable feeling. Charlie had said that he would be staying on the base that night so it wasn't because they hadn't heard from him. It was just a gut feeling that something was wrong, very wrong.

"He said that he was staying on the base tonight, so that we wouldn't have to bother picking him up," Jim said, trying to ignore the feeling.

"Yes, he did, Jim. We'll just have to wait until tomorrow and ask him if there was any trouble. I'm going to bed now. Good night Jim."

"Yeah, me too, Sparks. If anything were wrong we'd hear from the base, I'm sure."

The two men went off to their own rooms and settled in for the night. The call they were expecting never came.

The next morning the two men got up, dressed, had breakfast, and drove to the base. It was six o'clock when they arrived at the front gate.

They drove directly over to the squadron's hangar and reported in. Jim asked the duty officer if he had dispatched the duty driver to pick up Commander Boyle.

"No Lieutenant Commander, I didn't, I guess that means that you have not heard the news," the officer said rather frankly.

"What news, what's happened? Didn't the plane come back?"

"No, it didn't come back. We're not sure exactly what happened. All we know for sure is that they didn't come back and no one has heard from them. The captain is checking on it now. If you want to call him, maybe he can tell you more."

Jim Johnston reached for the phone to call Captain Wilson. Just as he had finished dialing the last digit, however, the captain walked through the door of the office. Jim hung up the phone.

"Captain Wilson, sir," he began, "good morning, Can you tell me, what is the status on Commander Boyle's plane?"

"I don't know, Lieutenant Commander. We had a report of a distress call from them at nine o'clock last night, but no one has heard from them since. Search and rescue has been notified, but we're not sure, even, where to start looking. We have their flight plan and an approximate fix on their position from their distress call, but the two don't agree. They were jamming at the time so we couldn't get a radar fix either."

"Captain, is there anything that we can do to help," Sparks asked.

"No, son, nothing; we've got work for the two of you to do and right now that's the most important thing that you can do."

"But Captain, perhaps we could take a plane and follow their flight plan to help look for them," Jim suggested.

"No, search and rescue is doing that already. They do it all the time, they'll find them if they are down. That is their job and they can do it a lot better than we can. Believe me."

Neither Jim nor Sparks wanted to argue with the captain. They had seen how stubborn he could be. The two men went out and tried to begin their training classes, but neither, had any confidence that the captain had been totally honest with them. The two men decided that they would go out on their own and look, after they got off duty that afternoon.

Time passed by very slowly for Jim and Sparks. The two men now realized that the feeling that they had had the night before was a premonition of danger for their friend. Anxiously they waited for the day to end. It seemed like the time would never pass, but it finally did.

Jim and Sparks went over to the Navy's Special Services department office and inquired about borrowing a small plane for a few hours. They were given permission and told where to pick up the craft.

They drove over to where the plane was parked and left their car. Jim walked around the plane and gave it a quick pre-flight check. He and Sparks got in and Jim started the engine. The plane was a small single engine Cessna; it had seats for four, which was more than adequate for their needs.

Jim put on the headset and turned on the radio.

"North Island tower, this is Cessna-One-Seven-Niner. Request take-off clearance and instructions, over?"

"Cessna-One-Seven-Niner, this is the tower. You are cleared for take-off on runway three left. What's your destination, over?"

"Tower, we are going to join in the search for the missing Navy A-3 aircraft, by following their flight plan, over,'"

"Roger, Cessna, Good luck. Over and out,"

Jim gunned the engine and began taxiing to runway three left. It sure was different than flying a jet, he thought to himself. The little Cessna took off easily and Jim had no trouble getting used to it. He had been an air circus pilot before joining the Navy, and all they ever had were prop planes. Jim took the little plane up to eight hundred feet, and began to follow the exact course that the A-3 was supposed to have gone the night before.

They flew at only eight hundred feet and a mere eighty miles an hour, searching the ground for any sign of wreckage. Sparks had a pair of binoculars, which he kept moving slowly back and forth very carefully.

Jim, likewise, was watching and skillfully searching his side of the ground. They flew in silence for about three hours, looking but not speaking, but to no avail. There wasn't a sign of anything out of the ordinary.

After five hours, the two men were both weary and discouraged and decided to return to base. They would come back out tomorrow and try again, following the course in reverse.

Jim turned the little plane for home. When they had landed and returned the plane, the two men drove silently back to the beach house and turned in for the night.

The next morning, when the two men had reported in for work, they received a message that Captain Wilson wanted to see them immediately, in his office. The two men, hopeful that the captain might have some good news for then, rushed to the captain's office,

The captain did not have good news, however; instead he reprimanded them for having gone out to search for the missing plane; he ordered them not to go out again. Both men were shocked by this attitude, and tried to protest. They were very quickly put down, and the captain made himself very clear that they were not to try disobeying or else they would be severely punished.

The two very disheartened men walked slowly out of the captain's office and headed for their respective assignments for the day.

The time passed very slowly for them and when at last the workday was over, they went home and got drunk.

CHAPTER EIGHT

On the side of a mountain, surrounded by trees in a forest of thick pines, was the wreckage of Commander Boyle's plane. It was not visible from the air and only visible on the ground from about fifty yards away. The wings had been sheared off in the crash, along with the wheels and tail.

The pilot had been killed instantly as a large tree branch came through the windshield. It was not a pretty sight. Charlie Boyle was alive, but both of his legs were broken and he could not move because some of the instruments had broken loose and were pinning him in his seat.

The radio operator had been unconscious for the first day and a half. His left collarbone was broken and he had a very bad cut just below his left eye.

Once he had regained consciousness and was able to determine what had happened, the radio operator began trying to find the other two men.

"Commander Boyle, Lieutenant Commander James," he called out in an anguished voice.

"Willis, this is Commander Boyle, are you okay?"

"Not really, Commander. I think my shoulder is busted and I'm bleeding; how about you and the Lieutenant Commander?"

"I'm pinned in and my legs are broken. I can't see him but I think Lieutenant Commander James is dead."

"I'11 try to get up there and help you sir, if I can."

"Please do, and hurry if you can, Willis."

Radioman Second class Jim Willis moved very slowly, as he painfully got out of his seat and headed forward. He dropped his parachute to the floor and went to try and help the other two men. He gently lifted his arm, at the wrist, and slowly made his way through the debris.

As he entered the cockpit and surveyed the damage, his eyes fell upon the dead Lieutenant Commander's body. He immediately vomited and turned his head the other way. There was a large tree limb sticking through the pilot's seat where the Lieutenant Commander's head had been.

As soon as he could regain control of himself, he turned to the commander. The equipment that had the commander pinned down would require two men, with good arms, to move under normal circumstances. These, however, were not normal circumstances. Willis gently put his left hand inside his shirt, to support his injured shoulder. He then put all of his strength into the other arm and tried to move the gear.

"Commander, please try to help from underneath. I know you haven't get much room to gain leverage, but maybe we can get it to budge if we work together."

Charlie Boyle began trying to lift the heavy objects from his chest. It wasn't much good though because they were very heavy, and both of the men were too weak from their injuries.

"It's no good, Willis. We just can't do it without help," the commander said in a very discouraged tone.

"Then we'll just have to get help, sir," the radioman replied.

The young radioman went back to the radio room and began trying to make some of the radio equipment work. He turned off the switches for the jammers and turned on all of the radios.

"Mayday, mayday, mayday; this is Radioman James Willis on board downed naval aircraft. Can anyone hear me, over?"

There was no response so he tried again. Still, there was no response, so he tried changing frequencies. The receiver crackled as he began to tune in a frequency on which someone was talking.

"Mayday, mayday, mayday; this is Radioman James Willis on board downed naval aircraft. Do you read me, over?"

The conversation at the other end continued, uninterrupted. Willis tried calling for help several more times but got the same results, no reply.

Willis went to the storage closet across from his seat a got out a couple of blankets. He went forward and put a blanket over Lieutenant Commander James' body and the other one over Commander Boyle, almost in tears.

"I couldn't raise anyone on the radio, sir. The antenna must have broken off in the crash. How are you doing, Commander?"

"Not too well, I'm afraid. I keep drifting in and out of consciousness, and my legs hurt really badly. How's your shoulder?"

"It hurts real badly, sir, but I think I can handle it for a little while longer."

The two men looked at each other in silence. Each one was wondering just how long they would be there before help arrived. Each one was afraid that he would die there, alone, on the side of that mountain.

Willis went back to the radio compartment and started looking through the wreckage, again, for something to use to establish communication with the outside world.

That night a severe thunderstorm passed through the area. Torrential downpours of rain and hail were pelting the men through the broken windows of the airplane. The thunder and lightening seemed worse than they actually were due to the weakened condition of the two survivors.

Willis went forward and took the blanket off of the dead pilot's body and used it to try to provide Commander Boyle with a little shelter from the rain.

A piercingly brilliant flash of blue white light nearly blinded both of the men. It was followed very quickly by the thunderous crash as the lightening bolt struck a tree about a hundred yards away from the plane. The tree was splint into several large pieces, all of which were on fire as they fell to the ground. The fire started to spread. Before long there were several other trees burning. It wouldn't take long until the whole hillside would be ablaze. Thick smoke rose into the sky as the wind blew the fire and smoke toward the northeast, away from the plane. Boyle and Willis were quite aware, however, that if the wind changed direction, they could be directly in the path of the fire in very short order.

High atop another mountain, about twenty miles away from the fire, a forest ranger, was standing fire watch in a tower, saw the flames and smoke. He reported the fire.

Because of its remote location, and the fact that it was not readily accessible from the ground, it was decided to let the fire burn a while longer and then try to put it out when it was easier to get to.

About two hours after the fire started, the wind began to turn the fire back around towards the West. Again, the alert ranger reported the direction of the fire and, again, it was decided to just watch. Someone figured that it might just come around in a complete circle and burn itself out. This had happened before and just watching it had saved a lot of money. After all, it was not worth all of the trouble to get people out of bed and transport them to a fire that does the work for them anyway. Besides, no one lived there, there were no lives in danger, which they knew of.

As the fire burned its way back toward the place where it had started, there was a loud explosion and the flames shot over a hundred feet into the air. The fire had found one of the sheared wings from the A3 and ignited its fuel tank. Several hundred gallons of high-octane jet fuel caused the fire to spread rapidly.

When the ranger saw the flash from the explosion and the resulting fireball, he immediately reported it to his supervisor. A helicopter was dispatched to survey the area in an attempt to find out what had caused the unusual explosion. Fire fighters were notified to get ready to be transported to the area.

It was almost an hour after the explosion before the helicopter arrived in the area of the reported fireball. The ranger directed its approach by radio from the tower.

Upon hearing the sound of the approaching helicopter, Willis tried again, in vain, to get out of the wreckage to wave for help. The door was smashed shut and the cockpit was too badly damaged for him to get out that way. Boyle, who was barely conscious, was able to reach a small, .38 caliber flare gun that he carried in his survival vest. He managed to pass it to Willis and instructed him to fire it out of the window and into the air. The noise from it being fired so close to his head was painful to his ears, but, if they were to be rescued, it was necessary.

In the fire tower, some twenty miles away, the ever-alert ranger saw the flare. The helicopter pilot saw it too.

"There is someone down there," the pilot radioed the ranger. "I'm going back for another look."

"Roger, Chopper One," the ranger replied, "I'll call for additional assistance."

The helicopter pilot turned around and flew back into the fire area. The ranger called, once again, his superiors on the phone and reported the flare.

Both the pilot and the observer scanned the ground thoroughly, trying to locate the source of the flare. The smoke cleared a little as the wind, once again changed direction and blew it and the fire away from the downed aircraft.

As the helicopter made its second pass directly over the plane, still unable to see very much other than trees and smoke, Willis fired a second flare out of the cockpit window.

The flare went up very close to the helicopter and the observer was able to get an excellent fix on its origin. The pilot tried, unsuccessfully, to make radio contact but when that failed he tried going lower and turned on the bright spotlight that was attached to the helicopter's belly. Slowly and methodically, the helicopter hovered over the circle of light as both crewmen strained to see anything man-made below them. Finally, the pilot saw the reflection of his light on something shiny.

"Definitely looks man-made from the reflection," he said to his companion. The observer agreed.

"Fire tower, this is chopper one. Do we have any reports of missing aircraft in this area?

"Wait one, I'll check."

The helicopter continued to hover over the wreckage while the ranger checked his logs and called the nearest airport.

"Air-Sea Rescue is looking for a missing Navy A3 about eighty miles southwest of here," the ranger reported back to the helicopter pilot. "Can you identify anything at all?"

"Negative. All I can be sure of is that there is something, most likely man-made by its reflection of my spotlight, down there. The trees and the smoke are too dense. I'm going to try the bull horn."

The chopper pilot got as close to the tops of the trees as he dared, while trying to keep the spotlight on the shiny object, and called out over his bullhorn, "This is the United States Forest service calling whoever is down there. We are trying to identify you and find a way to get you out; if you can, radio us on Tact Com Two." There was no response.

"If you don't have radio but are alive, try to signal."

A third flare rose from directly below.

"Chopper One to Ranger Station."

"Go ahead, Chopper One."

"There is definitely something and someone down there. They do not have the ability to establish radio communication but they responded to our last hailing. I'd guess it is definitely a plane and there is at least one survivor. There is no place for me to land and I am not equipped for airborne rescue. Recommend you notify Air-Sea Rescue immediately."

Almost as soon as the ranger station reported the findings to Air-Sea Rescue, a call was received at the Naval Air Station Duty Office. Air-Sea Rescue called to let them know that a downed aircraft had been found and that a rescue attempt was underway.

The duty officer called Captain Wilson at his home and reported what he had been told.

"Should I notify Commander Boyle's crew, sir," the duty officer asked.

"No, let's don't give them any false hope. They're already taking this pretty hard."

It was seven o'clock the next morning, when Jim Johnston and Sparks reported in, before either of them heard anything. A rumor had spread throughout the squadron that the plane had been found and that all on board were dead.

Deeply saddened and angry about the way they found out, Johnston and Sparks went to see Captain Wilson. He had, after all, promised to keep them informed.

"Captain Wilson, sir," Johnston said as soon as he saw the officer, "I've just learned that Commander Boyle's plane has been found and all aboard are dead. Is that true, sir," there was just a hint of his under-lying anger showing in the tone of his voice.

"No, Jim. It is not certain. We have a report, from a forest ranger in Nevada. They have found something in the middle of a forest fire that they think might be a plane. They think there is at least one survivor. They have been unable to positively identify anything or anyone because they haven't been able to get in close enough."

"But, why wasn't I informed, sir? You know how important this is to me."

"That is the very reason you weren't told, Jim. In case it isn't him. We just don't know enough of the facts. The location is about eighty miles northeast of where they should have been."

"I'd like your permission to fly over there and try to find out if it is them, sir."

"Request denied, Lieutenant Commander. I can't spare you to go out on what is most likely a wild goose chase."

"But Captain…" Johnston protested.

"That will be quite enough misters. I will have you placed under armed guard and confined to quarters if I have to."

"Aye, aye sir," Johnston replied. He turned and left the captain's office cursing silently.

Two air-sea rescue helicopters left their headquarters immediately after receiving the ranger's report. Both helicopters arrived at the fire scene and were attempting to find a way to get to the downed plane.

The density of the forest did not offer a clear landing area. The slope of the mountain and the fire further complicated things. It was decided that one chopper would attempt to lower a paramedic by cable into an area that was already well burnt out. The other helicopter would stand by with stretchers to be lowered by cable once the paramedic found the plane.

It was a fairly dangerous mission due to all of the hazards; but one for which these crews were well trained.

The pilot of chopper two-one found a spot that looked big enough to lower his man through and hovered over it. The crewman slowly descended into the area. As he neared the ground, he was able to see the airplane and called in a report. He could see a US Navy jet plane.

The paramedic released his harness as soon as he was on the ground and ran to the plane.

"Is anyone in there," he called, shinning his flashlight on the cockpit.

"Yes, we're here. Help us," Radioman Willis shouted in reply.

"I'll be right in."

The paramedic went all the way around the airplane, looking for a way in. The side door was smashed so badly that it couldn't be opened. The plane was lying flat on the ground, so the escape hatch on the underside was useless also. The back of the plane had been pretty well crushed by a couple of very large trees that had fallen on it.

At last, the paramedic climbed up one of the fallen trees and walked along the top of the fuselage until he reached the cockpit window.

"Good morning, gentlemen, how are you doing," he asked, as cheerfully as he could.

"A whole a lot better now that you're here," the commander replied.

The paramedic looked over the situation carefully and quickly summed up the situation.

"Chopper two-one, I'm going to need a lot of help down here; at least two more people, the Jaws of Life, a chainsaw, a couple of stretchers, and a body bag. I have two severely injured in the early stages of shock and one dead."

"Two-two, this is two-one. Please lower your paramedic and stretchers. We have Jaws of Life on board but not a chainsaw."

"Two-one, this is Forest Service helicopter. We have a chainsaw at the ranger station."

"Roger, Forest Service. Got any spare people?"

"We have a couple of fire fighters and a ranger there as well."

"Roger, two-one will pick up the chainsaw and one or two volunteers at the ranger station and return to this location."

"Two-two copies, our guy is on his way down now with the stretchers, Jaws of Life, and body bag."

Chopper two-one sped off toward the ranger station. Two-two lowered their paramedic and the needed supplies and the hovered overhead.

When the second paramedic was on the ground, he grabbed the Jaws of Life and one of the stretchers and jogged to the downed aircraft.

Together, the two paramedics worked from the cockpit window opening to try to cut a hole big enough for them to get in and get the injured men out. It took them almost an hour to finally get into the wreckage. During this time, two-one returned with more men, a chainsaw, and more medical supplies.

The first two paramedics were able to get in to the cockpit and wrestle the equipment off of Boyle's chest. They cut him loose from his seat and shoulder harness and put a cervical collar on him to immobilize his neck. Because Boyle was seated, they were unable to get him onto a backboard without moving him.

Two firefighters that had returned with the chainsaws began cutting away some of the trees and branches that had fallen on the plane and then went to cut a roughly hewn landing zone out of the burned out area. They feverishly cut down everything they could to a foot or less.

The two paramedics did their best to set broken bones, immobilize those that they could not set, and make the survivors as comfortable as possible for transport out of the crash site.

All the while, the wind driven fire was being blown in one direction and then another; first traveling away from the rescue effort and then back toward it. An air-borne fire fighting crew was called in for fire suppression around the rescue area. This worked to keep the fire far enough back to give the teams time to work. At last the injured were ready for transport.

Chopper two-one handled their extraction hovering about a foot from the ground in the cleared area. The rescue crew continued working to try to extract the body of the deceased pilot from the wreckage. He and the firefighters would be taken out by two-two.

Back at the naval base, a call came into the squadron duty office. The call brought both joy and sadness. Joy, because two men were alive; sadness because one had died.

Captain Wilson summoned Johnston and Sparks to his office.

"Commander Boyle is being flown to the hospital at Nellis Air Force Base, just outside of Las Vegas. You men have permission to go there if you wish."

"Yes sir, thank you sir," both men replied in unison.

Jim and Sparks left Wilson's office and went directly to Special Services and took the same plane they had borrowed previously and flew to Nellis. It was a happy reunion when they were at finally able to see their friend.

CHAPTER NINE

Commander Boyle and Radioman Willis were flown directly to a military hospital outside of Las Vegas, at Nellis Air Force Base. The body of the dead pilot was sent back to the squadron headquarters in California.

Jim Johnston and Sparks flew the same small Cessna that they had borrowed for their search. This time, however, they were much more hopeful. They flew to Nellis Air Force Base and then went to the hospital to visit their friend.

When they arrived at the hospital, they were informed of the commander's condition. Both of his legs were broken, he had three broken ribs, several cuts and bruises, and he was being treated for shock.

They were told that he would probably be hospitalized for two to three weeks and then released for limited duty. He would need some physical therapy and would not be allowed to fly for at least two months. They were only allowed to see him for ten minutes and only after they explained that they had flown all the way from San Diego to see him.

Boyle had both legs in casts and in traction. He was bandaged like a mummy, practically, and he was only semi-conscious due to his pain medication.

The two men left the hospital with mixed emotions. They were glad that their friend was alive and sad for his condition.

The two men flew back to California. They had to return the plane. On their trip back, they decided to drive back up in the morning.

Charlie Boyle had only been partially conscious during the flight to the hospital. The morphine that the paramedic had given him had knocked him out. Upon awakening in the hospital, he was startled by his surroundings. The nurse, seeing that he was awake and disoriented, spoke softly and reassured him. She told him where he was and how he had gotten there.

"What about the other two men who were with me," he queried. "There was only one, Commander, a young man by the name of Willis. He is in another room down the hall," she replied softly.

"No, there were two men. The pilot and the radioman," he said, troubled and confused.

"I don't know about the pilot," she said, "we only received word that you and the radioman were coming here."

After reassuring him that she would find out what had become of the pilot, the nurse was able to get Charlie to rest quietly once again.

It was almost ten p.m. by the time Johnston and Sparks drove back to the hospital. They were told that visiting hours had ended at nine o'clock and they they'd have to come back in the morning.

They found a room at a nearby motel for the evening and went right to sleep.

At seven a.m., the two drove back to the hospital and were told that they'd have to wait until nine o'clock for visiting hours before they could see their friend.

When visiting hours finally began, they went up to see Boyle.

Charlie Boyle was awake and in reasonably high spirits, considering what he had just been through and the condition that he was in. He did not remember what had happed to the pilot. He was quite pleased when he saw his friends walk into the room.

"Well, it's about time," he said as they walked in, "I was wondering what happened to you two."

"We were here to see you yesterday, but you were out of it."

"But they told me that my radioman was brought in with me. That he was in a room down the hall."

"Not I, Skipper, the guy who was with you in the plane is named Willis. He's down the hall," Sparks informed him.

"Oh yeah, now I remember, I think," Boyle said, unconvincingly.

Jim told Charlie about their flight up the day before and how they had flown back and then driven up.

"Well, what about the guys I was with then? What happened to them?

The nurse told me that only one came here with me. Do you know anything about the other?"

Sparks looked curiously at Jim, who looked equally puzzled back at him. They both looked at Charlie.

"You don't remember," Sparks asked, hesitating a moment.

"Remember what?'

"No one has told you and you don't remember, Charlie," Jim asked.

"No, Jim, nobody has told me anything other than the radioman is down the hall. All I remember is taking off from North Island yesterday and waking up here today. I know there were two men with me when I took off but I don't know who they are or where they are. Now you guys tell me that it wasn't you that were with me and you give me dumb ass looks and beat around the bush. Now, will one of you please tell me what is going on?"

His voice was beginning to rise and the nurse had told them not to get him too overly excited.

"Ok, Charlie," Jim began, "just take it easy and I'll tell you. You're pretty busted up and they don't want you getting too riled up. Okay?"

Boyle shook his head and calmed down a bit.

"Well, you and two other men took off from North Island, four days ago, not yesterday. Your plane crashed into the side of a mountain, not too far from here, but about eighty miles off course. The pilot was killed. You were trapped in your seat, under a bunch of equipment for a couple of days. The radioman is alive. He is down the hall with some cuts and bruises and a broken collarbone. The both of you are very lucky to be alive."

"You mean that all of this happened over a period of several days and I don't remember any of it?"

"That's right, Skipper," Sparks said. "We thought that we had lost you for a while there."

About this time, a very pretty nurse came in. She told them that they would have to leave. It was time for the commander's sponge bath.

Charlie was released from the hospital after only four days. He would be in a wheelchair for quite some time though, until his ribs healed enough for him to get around on crutches.

Johnston and Sparks were waiting outside, to take him back to California. It was a hero's welcome that he received when he got back to the squadron headquarters. Willis had gotten in a couple of days earlier and had hailed him as the hero of all times for using the flare gun to get them rescued.

Charlie didn't remember any of what Willis said had happened.

Captain Wilson welcomed him back and told Boyle and Johnston to take the next week off. Sparks, however, had to go back to work with the enlisted men. Wilson wanted each of them, Sparks included, to go through the aircrew survival training course again. He said he wanted them to take the refresher since many of them had completed the course years before.

That evening, when Sparks got back to the beach house, the three men enjoyed a happy reunion.

"You know, Skipper, you guys gave us a bad scare," Sparks said.

"Yeah, I can imagine, from what you've been telling me. It must have been scary. I really can't remember any of it, which is probably a good thing. But, why didn't you come looking for us?"

Jim related the events that had unfolded. How, upon learning of the crash, second-handedly, they had borrowed the Cessna and then been grounded by Captain Wilson for going out on their own. Jim told him how cold, insensitive, and uncaring the Captain had been during the entire ordeal.

Sparks explained how the Captain had even threatened them with being arrested to keep them from joining the search.

Boyle was deeply troubled to hear his friends saying all of these things. He knew that they must be true though, because he trusted them. They were his only real friends.

That night, when they turned in for the night, all three of the men were totally disgusted with the Navy, their captain, and the raw deal that life had given them in California.

It was no surprise, to Sparks, the next morning, when Jim announced at breakfast, that he had had another of his strange dreams.

"Did you write it down?" Sparks asked.

"Yes, I did. This one's a real gem too."

Jim started describing his dream in detail. Charlie, until now, had always tried to shut him up when he started with this but not this time. He listened intently.

"What about the airlines," Sparks asked.

"Yes, the missing piece," Jim replied, "that's the part that finally made sense in this dream. You, Sparks, go to Los Angeles and get a job working for them, fixing radios on the jumbos."

"Sure, why didn't I think of that before," Sparks exclaimed, "that has to

happen in order to put the whole thing together; But how? I can't just waltz right in there and tell them who I really am and land a job."

"That's another part of it. You give them the name of your friend who was on the cargo plane. By the time they check it, we'd be done and gone anyway."

Charlie's interest was peaked now, "what in the world are you two going on about?"

"Remember a while back, Skipper, Jim was talking about that remote controlled hijacking and the dreams he'd been having," Sparks offered.

"Yeah, I remember. I told him he was crazy."

"Crazy as a fox, Charlie," Jim retorted.

"Well, I suggested that he write them down so that we could talk about them and study them. He's been doing that for the past couple of weeks and we've discovered some pretty fantastic stuff."

"Go ahead, Sparks, tell him the whole thing," Jim encouraged.

"And what, pray-tell is that? The remote controlled hijacking of a 747," Charlie asked rhetorically.

"Exactly Skipper," Sparks replied.

"Well, I must be crazy too, Sparks, but I want to hear it. Go ahead, give it to me."

Sparks was really surprised at Charlie's willingness to listen. He started to spell out the whole plan, as he understood it. Jim interjected pieces that Sparks was unsure of. When Sparks had finished, Boyle offered his opinion.

"That sounds like a good plan, guys, but I see a few flaws."

Charlie went on to elaborate. There were many ways in which the plan could fail, but, he had to admit, there were many ways in which the whole thing could work.

The three men talked for several hours, discussing the pros and cons of

many of the facets of the elaborate idea. It was after two a.m. when they finally turned in for the night. Sparks had to go to work the next day, so he went to sleep quickly. The two officers were both awake in their rooms for several hours, mulling ideas over in their minds.

Charlie's casts came off after seven weeks. During that time, the three men had many discussions about the hijacking idea. Jim and Sparks had had to work, leaving Charlie alone all day to sit and think, think and sit, and ponder. He began jotting notes down in a notebook and then discussing them with the other two in the evenings. He looked at the entire idea as a military planning exercise.

Because his muscles had not been used while the casts were on, Charlie was sent to a physical therapist to get his legs back into shape. He welcomed the pain as he worked the legs to tone and strengthen the muscles.

Finally, the flight surgeon gave him permission to return to duty.

The Naval Board of Inquiry's investigation of the mountainside crash had shown that he had not been at fault since he had been the copilot at the time of the crash; but, they harshly criticized him for not doing more to prevent the crash since he was the senior pilot in the airplane. Charlie Boyle was ordered to resume full-time active duty once again, with a letter of reprimand in his personnel folder. Training the other pilots to fly tactical missions against the "enemy" and doing it without being detected by radar was a job that he was the best at.

One day, after completing their respective training sessions, Charlie Boyle and his roommates took their own plane up for a "refresher" flight. At least, that is how he justified it with Captain Wilson. It was actually a chance to discuss their plan without interruption and to take a look around.

Charlie had asked Jim for the location of the barn that he had seen in one of his dreams. Together, they had determined that it was located at the site of an old movie location, about eighty miles from Phoenix, in the desert. Jim wasn't sure, but thought that it was accessible by air. They were going to check it out. Charlie followed Jim's guidance and flew the plane east towards the movie set.

When they finally saw the site, they flew around it in a low circle, looking for signs of anyone being there; they realized that it was the same place where they had seen the wreck of the Cessna on their way west. They saw no sign of activity anywhere nearby so Charlie landed the A3 and taxied to the barn. The trio deplaned and went exploring.

The barn was actually quite large. It had been built to look like a barn from the 1800's but, in actuality; it was more like a modern warehouse. There were two large doors, on the backside of the building, that were big enough to drive their plane inside. A smaller door, with a broken pad lock on it, allowed them access to the inside. Each of the men, upon entering the building, went off in a different direction to explore. They returned to the plane two hours later.

After they took off, the three men talked about what they had seen and found during their visit.

They flew back to North Island, put the plane back into its hangar, and then went home for the night.

"As I see it, there are still several issues to work out," Charlie said on the ride back to the beach house, "like how would the ransom money be picked up. The authorities would be all over it like bees on honey. That is, to say, if the airline would even pay it."

"I'm sure they'd pay it," Sparks offered.

"Having them deliver it would be out of the question; So would picking it up in person," Jim said.

"This one will require more thought," Charlie said.

"Maybe Jim will have another dream," Sparks joked.

The trio sat around the kitchen table and discussed several ideas and drank beer for a couple of hours. Then, Jim remembered something that he'd see in the desert.

"I've got it," He exclaimed. "At the movie set, there was a two-seat Cessna in the back of the barn. It looked like a camera plane because I noticed cameras on the wings, belly, and tail. We could rig it for remote control, fly it in a day or two ahead of time, and when we were ready, we could tell them to put the money in it and fly it out of there. We could threaten to blow up the airliner if they follow the plane and we could monitor that with the cameras."

"Sure," Sparks said, "I could vector the camera outputs to the blind carrier frequency that we are using for the remote control and we could see everything that was going on in and around the plane."

"But what if they try to sabotage the plane or follow it," Boyle insisted.

"They won't if they know we mean business and are willing and able to blow up the 747."

"Fine, Sparks," Charlie questioned, "but how do we convince them that we are both serious and capable of blowing up the plane?"

Jim handled the answer to this one, "Charlie, in one of my dreams I saw Sparks with a remote control box. He started up an airline fuel truck and crashed it into the terminal and blew it up."

"But then you'd be killing a bunch of innocent people," Charlie objected, "and they'd be even more determined to catch us."

"Okay, so we could give them a five minute warning to get the people out of there. You know, like a bomb threat."

"That might work," Charlie said, holding his chin in his hand, deeply engrossed in thought.

The three men spent a great deal of time over the next several weeks thinking and planning. Each one looked at the entire scenario from different points of view. The two officers used their training in military strategy while Sparks looked at things from a technical perspective. They spent many nights discussing their ideas and formulating a plan. The list of resources that they would need grew longer each day. The hardest things to procure, they reasoned would be the things they needed the most; explosives, a truck, a plane or two. Slowly but steadily they plodded through the seemingly endless ideas. Separately as well as together the three men made up lists of things that they would need. They also critiqued each other's ideas looking for risks as well as rewards to each. They came to the conclusion that there were an awful lot of things that they needed that they had no idea where they would get the resources.

One day, some weeks later, Jim decided to drive out to the desert to take another look at the movie set they had found. He had a couple of days off and the weather was supposed to be reasonably decent.

He got into his car and headed east on Interstate Route eight toward Yuma. He stopped in Coyote Wells for gas and a cold drink and continued his eastward trek. When he passed the intersection with route eighty-six, leading toward El Centro he realized that there were military installations along their planned flight path. That would probably require some rethinking.

He was about halfway between Aztec and Sentinel when his car began to overheat. The red warning light on the dashboard flashed a couple of times and then came on and stayed lit. He eased the Camaro off the road and onto the shoulder. Then he turned off the engine. He got out and opened the hood. Steam was already pouring out of the hole in the radiator hose. The hose had suddenly worn out and ruptured. The hole had caused him to lose all of his coolant and the car to overheat.

There were no other cars to be seen. He was stranded. A pair of F-14's from El Centro, Jim guessed, flew over at about twelve thousand feet. They weren't much help to the stranded motorist. It was nearly three hours before Jim spotted another car, a beat up Chevy Suburban. As the vehicle pulled off the road, on to the shoulder, Jim could see that the driver was an elderly man, probably in his early seventies. His long gray hair was pulled back into a ponytail. The old man had on a denim vest and blue jeans. He wore some turquoise jewelry and a sweaty red bandana.

"What seems to be the problem, young fellow?"

"The radiator hose busted and no water."

"That's bad. Nearest gas station is about thirty-five miles; over in Theba. I can't take you today; maybe tomorrow. You're welcome to stay at my place for the night. Taint much, just an old trailer but it keeps the rattlers out of your bunk at night."

"Thank you, sir," was the only reply Jim could come up with.

Jim and the old man got into the truck and drove off. The old man told Jim that his name was Walking Buffalo, he was a full-blooded Cherokee. He had chosen not to live on the Ak-Chin reservation and because he was nearly one hundred years old, no one tried to stop him.

Walking Buffalo drove east on Interstate eight until they came to a small dirt road on the right that led off into the desert. He turned the truck on to the dirt road and pressed the accelerator to the floor. The old truck's engine sputtered and coughed a couple of times and then roared to life. They bounced across the desert floor and an amazing speed of about thirty-five miles per hour.

After a bone-crunching ride, which had lasted nearly an hour, they pulled up in front of an aluminum camping trailer. Jim guessed that it was probably thirty or forty years old. There were very few traces of paint on it and all of the tires were flat. There were two twenty-pound propane bottles on the front of it but they were so rusty that he suspected they were empty. A scrawny old hound dog, asleep under a corner of the trailer, stirred, but didn't get up, as the truck pulled up.

When the two men got out, Jim noticed a couple of old trucks a short distance away. Walking Buffalo saw him looking at them and said, "There might be a hose on one of those trucks that would work on your car. We'll look at them in the morning."

"Walking Buffalo, I don't suppose you'd have a telephone out here, would you?"

"No need; no one to call. Family is all dead."

The next morning, at precisely six a.m., Jim was awakened by an unfamiliar sound. As he stumbled out of bed and into the living room, Jim saw Walking Buffalo kneeling out front, facing the sunrise and chanting in his native tongue. Jim waited, respectfully, until the old man finished his morning prayer.

After a cup of breakfast coffee, the two men went out to the old trucks. They found a universal hose that looked to be in usable condition. The old man removed it and the two clamps holding it in place and the two departed to go to fix Jim's car.

Once the car was fixed, Jim offered Walking Buffalo some money but the old man refused.

"We are put on this earth to help others when they are in need. You can repay me by doing the same for someone else when the time comes," Walking Buffalo said. The two men shook hands and Jim drove away.

Once Jim arrived at the movie set, he found several smaller buildings that they had not seen from the air. One was a small concrete-block structure sitting by itself about two hundred yards away from all of the others. It was painted red and had a large sign on it forbidding smoking within five hundred feet. Upon closer inspection, Jim found that it was an explosive storage shed.

Jim searched the entire area. He found several cars, some motorcycles, movie props, cameras, lights, costumes, dummies and all sorts of other gadgets. Jim went to each building and made a list of the things that would be useful to them as well as a note to remind himself which building each thing was in.

Jim left the site and drove back to the beach house. When he arrived, neither of the other two men expected the news he brought back with him.

"I've got the answer to the camera problem," he began. "We can use small video tape cameras, like these," he said proudly displaying the cameras he'd found. "Explosives won't be a problem either. There is a shed full of them out there."

"Where exactly did you get these, Jim," Boyle asked with a touch of hostility in his voice.

"In one of the buildings at the movie set."

"Great and just what if someone goes looking for them while we are planning all of this? If they find things are missing, they are likely to post a guard. Then what," Charlie's tone was even more hostile this time.

The three men discussed whether or not they should put the cameras back. They decided not to, since that might draw even more attention to their activities at the set.

Sparks had an idea of where and how to get a truck. They could rent one from a rental agency a few days before they were going to "crash". That way, once they were presumed dead, no one would bother looking for the truck.

The hardest part, they all figured, was how Sparks could get a job working for the airlines? That was the key to the whole operation and it was a question that they could not answer.

Sparks, it was decided, would take two weeks leave. He would go to Los Angeles and try to get a job with an airline. If he were successful, the "crash" would take place a week later.

Captain Wilson was reluctant to grant Sparks the time off, stating that Sparks was too valuable and that training time had been curtailed too much already. Boyle interceded for Sparks. He offered to take on Sparks' classes. Wilson finally agreed and approved the request.

Sparks left that evening for Los Angeles.

He had very little trouble getting a job as a maintenance technician on 747-radio equipment. His knowledge was unmistakable and the hardest part was actually getting the interview.

Sparks assumed the identity of his friend, Gerry, who had been killed in the crash in Virginia. After all, by the time anyone could check on him, he'd be gone, so he thought.

Now the only problem was getting the small plane and the explosives into the airport.

Sparks worked for a week and a half for the airline. Then one morning,

he reported to his crew chief that he would need a couple of week's leave of absence. The crew chief was very hesitant to grant his request and wanted to know why he wanted a leave after so short of an employment.

"Jobs are hard to find, chief, and I had to take this one when it became available. I need to go into the hospital for a minor surgical procedure and then come back once it's healed."

Sparks was a very convincing liar, when he had to be. He convinced the crew chief to give him a leave of absence, without pay of course, for up to three weeks.

Sparks returned to San Diego using one of his free trips as an airline employee.

While Sparks had been gone, Jim and Charlie had managed found more than a pound and a half of plastic explosives in the storage shed at the movie set. The next step was to get the truck.

Early on Friday morning, shortly after dawn, the crew of Alpha-Papa-Seven-Three-Zero got into their plane. This was scheduled to be a routine training flight. Commander Boyle had requested the opportunity to take his crew up, on a "refresher" mission. They were going to stage an attack on an aircraft carrier off the coast of California.

As they taxied down the runway, the three men took their last look at the nightmare that they had been forced to endure for the past several months.

It was a feeling of escape, an exhilarating joy at being free from all of this, which they were feeling as the A-3 slipped quickly from the view of those on the ground.

CHAPTER TEN

As soon as they were airborne, Charlie put the plane on the course headed toward the "target" ship. It was about a hundred and fifty miles off the coast of California.

Sparks flipped the switches for the jammers, as usual. They hummed softly as they began to warm up.

"The jammers are warming up, Skipper."

"Roger Sparks. As soon as they are ready, we'll put our plan into operation. There's still time to back out gentlemen."

Sparks and Johnston both voiced their willingness to continue with the plan.

It didn't take long for the equipment to be ready to use. Sparks activated the jammers and reported to Boyle when it was done.

"Okay guys, here goes," Charlie said as he reset his radio dial to the Guard Frequency that they were not allowed to jam.

"Mayday, Mayday, Mayday. This is Navy Alpha-Papa-Seven-Three-Zero calling Mayday," Charlie spoke into his microphone.

It took him three attempts, repeating the distress call, before he could raise anyone on the radio. Things on the ground were in a panic, due to the jammed radar.

"Alpha-Papa-Seven-Three-Zero, this is San Diego tower, over," called the frantic voice of an aircraft controller.

As Charlie put the plane into a gradual turn to the East, he repeated his distress call.

"Mayday, Mayday, Mayday. This is Navy Alpha-Papa-Seven-Three-Zero. We are in trouble. San Diego, do you copy, over?"

"Alpha-Papa-Seven-Three-Zero, this is San Diego tower. We copy you, what is the nature of your problem, over?"

"We've taken a bird strike in our port engine. It is on fire and our fire suppression has failed, over."

With that, Charlie dropped the plane down to fifty feet above the water and signaled Sparks to jam the guard frequency also.

Sparks flipped another switch. This made static appear in their headsets, indicating that now even the last channel was being jammed.

After about thirty seconds, Sparks opened the switch and stopped jamming the guard frequency. The three men listened to the sound of their own disappearance.

"Alpha-Papa-Seven-Three-Zero, this is San Diego tower, do you read me, over."

The controller repeated his call several more times, but Charlie didn't answer.

"Alpha-Papa-Seven-Three-Zero, where are you? Answer me for Pete's sake."

The frantic calls from the tower went unanswered by the crew of the now "missing" plane known as Alpha-Papa-Seven-Three-Zero.

"Well, now they'll be looking for us. They will have Air-Sea rescue out here within the hour so we'll head straight for the barn," Charlie said smiling, with a sense of pride at how smoothly things had gone so far.

Charlie switched the transponder to the setting for a 747 airliner and climbed to twenty-seven thousand feet and flew directly toward their desert hideout. Sparks kept the jammers going all the while.

"This is San Diego tower calling Air-Sea Rescue, over."

"San Diego tower, this is Air-Sea Rescue, over."

"Air-Sea Rescue, this is San Diego tower, be advised that we have an aircraft missing and presumed down, over."

Charlie Boyle landed the jet flawlessly on the hard packed dirt road and taxied up to the barn. Jim and Sparks got out and opened the barn doors and guided Charlie as he folded the A-3's wings and then carefully taxied the plane into the barn. Once they were safely inside, Charlie shut down the engines. They turned off all of the jammers and all but one of the radio receivers. They listened as normalcy resumed in the "outside" world.

There were dozens of calls reporting "near misses" during the blackout. It had reached as far as New Mexico and no one knew why. There were no reports of anyone sighting them.

The air traffic controller at North Island, as well as the one at San Diego, tried several more times to raise the missing plane on the radio; they finally gave up. The Navy air traffic controller reported the A-3's disappearance to Air-Sea Rescue. He reported that no one was sure of the plane's location, but informed them of the proposed flight plan and planned operation with the USS Enterprise off the coast of California. He also notified the aircraft carrier's captain. Air-Sea Rescue agreed to coordinate with the carrier since they were probably closer and could, possibly, reach them faster. Twelve planes and several helicopters were dispatched from the ground based search and rescue squadron and the ship's captain promised as much air support as he could. In all, more than thirty aircraft joined in the search.

Charlie and Jim listened for a quite a while and then switched off the radio. Charlie looked at Jim and Sparks with a smile of satisfaction; they had done well. They had successfully carried out the first phase of their plan.

"Sparks, you had better get going back to LA. We don't want you to be late for your new job Monday, now do we?"

"Right Skipper, what about you two though? How will I reach you if I have to?"

"It might be best if we get in touch with you, Sparks," Jim said.

"Yeah, until we find a place to stay, we'll be here and there's no phone, "Charlie added.

"Okay, but don't be strangers. We dead men don't have any friends except each other now," Sparks said, taking his flight suit off and changing into civilian clothes.

Jim took Sparks to a back corner of the barn to a spot where he had discovered several cars. Most of them were "distressed" movie props but a couple of them ran and even had valid California license plates on them. Sparks found the keys for a blue Chevy Nova above the driver's side sun visor; he started it up. The sound of a powerful engine surprised both men; Jim opened the hood. From the size of the powerful V-8 engine, Jim guessed that this must be a car used in a chase scene. He closed the hood and Sparks backed it out the barn door.

"Better watch your speed, Sparks; we can't have you getting busted on your way back to Los Angeles," Jim chided.

"Right you are, Jim, I think this thing might have some get up and go to it, from the sound of the engine."

"Sure sounds that way."

Sparks left the movie set and drove towards Yuma, a sign on the side of the road said that it was twenty miles. Sparks tried the radio, the only station it could receive was a farm station which was reporting the cost of pork bellies and grain and feed costs. He turned the radio off and drove in silence.

Jim and Charlie drove up to the movie house in one of the other cars that Jim had found in the barn.

"Tomorrow we'll change the numbers on the Cessna and start stripping the A-3," Charlie said.

"What about a truck," Jim asked.

"Well, I figure we can do one of two things. We can either rent one or steal one. We haven't got a whole lot of money, so stealing one may be the best answer. We could probably grab one at a truck stop while the driver is in the bathroom. By the way, Jim, did you search every building here? I don't suppose they would have left a trailer truck here."

"I found several cars, a couple of motorcycles, and the plane but I haven't seen any sign of a truck."

"Well, if we end up having to steal one, we'll have to repaint it and smear mud all over the plates; maybe Sparks could grab us another set of plates in California."

The two men got out of the car and went into the movie house. It wasn't much more than a shell; it had been used as a prop from the outside only.

There were a couple of cots and some blankets amidst of the movie making paraphernalia; they were dusty from sitting there for a long time.

The two men spent the night there. The next morning they drove into Yuma and found a restaurant for breakfast.

After breakfast, the two men took a drive around the town to look things over. They had spotted a truck stop a few miles outside of town. There were a couple of motels, a Wal-Mart, a few grocery stores, and a good-sized shopping center near by.

Finally, they drove back to the movie set and each one took a motor cycle and rode around the location to see what else they could find. They searched for two hours before meeting up back at the barn; neither found a truck suitable for their needs.

That night, the two men drove to the truck stop that they had seen, about fifteen miles from the movie set. There was a small motel there and several trucks that were parked for the night.

They watched to see if anyone was around. One truck pulled in to the refueling point and the driver got out and filled his tanks. The driver put the pump nozzle back on its holder and went in to the store to pay; then he drove off. There was no one else to be seen.

Jim got out of the car and worked his way through the shadows and darkness until he got to where the trucks were parked. Charlie drove into the truck stop and filled the car up with gas. Then he walked in and talked to the clerk while he took his time to pay.

While the clerk was distracted, Jim went from rig to rig looking for a truck whose driver was not sleeping in the truck instead of the motel. He finally found one, a Kenworth. The keys were, of course, gone, but nothing else was locked. All he would have to do would be to hot wire the ignition and drive it away, if, he didn't get caught in the act first.

Quickly, quietly, and carefully, Jim went to work on the ignition wires. He found the necessary wires and cut them. He twisted two of the halves together and started the truck.

The sound of a truck starting up and driving away in the middle of the night was not unusual to the drivers who were asleep in their trucks, so no one paid any attention to Jim as he drove the rig out of the motel's driveway. No one, that is, except Charlie Boyle.

Once the truck had pulled out of the driveway and was gone from sight, Charlie paid for his gas and the bag full of junk food he had picked up and left. Charlie started his car and pulled out of the driveway and headed in the opposite direction of the truck. About a mile away from the truck stop, he turned around and drove past the motel and straight to the movie set. No one appeared to be following either one of them.

Both men drove quickly back to the movie set where they hid the truck in the barn with the plane. The trailer, however, had to be left outside because it was too big to fit with the plane inside the barn.

The next morning, the two officers decided to look over their prey. They used a pair of bolt cutters to remove the padlock from the back doors of the trailer. The trailer was only about half full. The plain white cartons that were encased in clear plastic shrink-wrap had no visible printing on any of them.

Jim searched around, on the six pallets, until he found a small red envelope that was labeled "Packing List Enclosed". He opened it and read it.

"Boy-oh-boy, do I know how to pick them or do I know how to pick them," Jim exclaimed proudly, "its paint, spray paint. There are two hundred and forty cases of spray paint here."

"Yeah, but what color, Jim?" Can we use them that is the important question? May I see the packing slip please," he said, looking over the packing slip Jim handed him.

"There are sixty cases of "School Bus Yellow," thirty five cases of "Flat Black," twenty five cases of "Red," and sixty cases of "Clear Enamel." Those aren't much good to us."

"Yeah, but the rest are. Look here; there are thirty cases of beige and thirty more of brown. We can paint the truck brown and the trailer beige. We can use the red, black, and yellow on the Cessna."

"You're right, Jim. You certainly did pick the right truck." The two men began unloading the paint cartons. They carried them into the barn and stored them, together by color, in one of the horse stalls. They opened each one and sprayed the flap with one of the cans inside to help them find the color they wanted when they started to use them.

The two men worked for much of the day, unloading the cartons, marking the boxes, and storing them in the barn.

They decided to repaint the Cessna first. After this, they would fly it to Los Angeles and contact Sparks, to fill him in on their acquisition of the truck and their need for different license plates. They also planned to give him the phone number for the cell phone that they had found in the cab of the truck.

The work was tedious; everything had to be done just right. The two men worked long into the night repainting the little plane. They painted it a very nice shade of red. Jim cut some stencils out of paint cartons, to use to paint the registration numbers on the sides, right over the place here the old ones had been.

Once the red paint was dried, Jim carefully held the stencils in place while Charlie took a can of yellow paint and sprayed the new numbers on one side of the plane.

"Where did you get these numbers, Jim," Charlie asked him, as he finished spraying over the stencil for a second time.

"We'll be safe with those numbers because the plane registered to those numbers is sitting in my mother's back yard, being used as a flower planter. It was my first plane and I just didn't have the heart to get rid of it."

"A flower planter," Charlie laughed in reply.

"Yes, she didn't know what else to do with it when I brought it home and then joined the Navy."

"We'll have to get Sparks out here to wire the cameras into the transceiver and get the remote control equipment working in this thing," Charlie told Jim.

By the time they finished it was about two o'clock in the morning. The two men had completely repainted the small plane and changed its registration numbers. The cameras would give them all around visibility when they used the plane. It was now time to get some sleep.

The next morning, which was Monday, the two men were a bit slow to rise. It was almost noon before they got to work on the truck. Today they would cover all of the chrome so that they could repaint the truck.

It took almost six hours to cover the spots that they didn't want painted. By six that evening they were ready to start painting the cab. Jim took a couple of cases of brown paint and started on the roof. It seemed almost a waste of effort to paint a part of the truck that no one would see; but they figured it was better to be safe than to be spotted from the air. Charlie took a couple of cases and started on the hood. They worked until they were just too tired to continue and decided to finish up in the morning.

It took Jim and Charlie all of the next several days to finish painting both the cab and the trailer, but when they finished even the real owner wouldn't be able to recognize it.

On Saturday afternoon, Jim took the Cessna and flew to the Orange County airport to contact Sparks. He landed there because it wasn't too far from Los Angeles and it offered some anonymity. They had to get word to him about the things they needed. They would also need to have him come out for a few days.

Jim called the airline's avionics maintenance shop and asked to speak to Joe Greene. He was told that there was no one there by that name. It took Jim a couple of minutes to think of a way to correct his mistake. He'd used Sparks' real name instead of the assumed name.

"Well, of course there isn't," Jim said acting as if he had been drinking, "that's my name. I'm looking for my brother, Gerry. Gerry Greene."

It took a couple of minutes but then Sparks' voice came on the line.

"Hello. Hello, Joe," Sparks said.

"Sorry, Sparks," Jim said, "I forgot your name for a minute. We need to meet tonight. You know how to get to Hollywood and Vine? Let's meet at 8:30."

"Ok, Joe," Sparks said and the line went dead.

When Sparks finished work for the day, he got into his car and drove to Hollywood and Vine. He saw Jim waiting near a hot dog vendor's cart. He pulled up, Jim got in, and they sped off.

Once they were safely on the road and away from the possibly of anyone overhearing them, Jim told Sparks about the truck, the Cessna, and the paint jobs on each.

"We've got just about everything we need to get ready on our side but we'll need you to install, wire and test the equipment. How are things going here? Oh, I almost forgot, we need you to steal a set of plates off of a tractor-trailer rig."

"Well, I've got a job with the airline, as you know, and that is going well so far. I've got the freedom to go anywhere in the airport that I need to, except for the tower."

"You shouldn't have to get in there anyway, so that should not present a problem."

"What about radio equipment and explosives, Jim? Have you figured out how to get them to me?"

"Well, Sparks, we've come up with a couple of alternatives. We could pack them in coffee grounds to throw off the scent of any dogs in the post office and mail them to your apartment a little at a time or we could fly them in, in the Cessna. What do you think? Could you get them out of the plane with out arousing suspicion?"

Sparks thought for a few moments. He suggested that Jim could radio that he was having engine trouble and request to land at LAX. He could request Sparks be sent to fix it, through the tower. They discussed this option and then ruled it out. Someone might connect him with the incident after they had taken the 747.

The pair finally decided that Jim would fly the stuff in to Orange County airport the following Saturday and then just carry the packages out to Sparks' waiting car. Sparks told Jim that he would have the license plates by then too. They drove back to the Cessna and Jim flew back to the desert. Jim briefed Charlie on his arrival back at the movie set.

The two men spent the next week removing all of the electronics gear from the A-3 and mounting it on racks in the semi's trailer. Charlie designed an antenna system that could be raised or lowered on the roof of the trailer. All they needed was for Sparks to come out and wire everything together.

Jim carefully extracted the explosive materials and detonators from the storage shed on the site. He wrapped everything in food canning jars and brown paper that he had found in the barn. He wrote detailed instructions for Sparks to follow on how to use it when the time came. The explosives were then placed in a plain brown cardboard box in a cool, dry corner of the barn.

By the time the following Saturday came around, the packages containing the necessary radio parts and the explosives were all ready for delivery.

Charlie and Jim loaded the boxes into the Cessna's storage compartment and then they flew to Orange County airport.

Sparks met them at the airport; they transferred their cargo to the trunk of his car and then drove away.

When they arrived at Sparks' apartment, they carried everything inside. After looking everything over, Sparks asked the two men if they'd care to spend the night or even the weekend before going back to the desert. They decided to stay.

Sparks spent the rest of the day putting the radio receivers together. He told the others that he would not be able to fully test them without a plane.

"How about the one for the car, Sparks?" Charlie asked. "The receiver for the car doesn't have to do as much as the two for the planes, Charlie. I'd feel a lot more comfortable if we could test those thoroughly."

The officers agreed. The radio receivers would be tested on the Cessna in the desert. That would also give Sparks some time to connect and test everything in the semi trailer. Sparks would take a couple of days off and fly to Phoenix where the others could pick him up.

"I'll tell my boss that my mother passed away and that will give me three days off. It doesn't cost me anything to fly, since I work for the airline. You guys can pick me up in Phoenix and we can test out everything we've got so far."

The three men drove out to the airport on Sunday afternoon. Charlie carried with him the new license plates for the truck and trailer. Sparks had found them quite easy to get. They also took the boxes with the radio receivers back with them. Sparks told them that he would be on the afternoon flight to Phoenix the next day. The two officers climbed aboard the Cessna and took off.

Monday morning dawned gray and cloudy in Los Angeles. The pollution index was off the charts. Phoenix was sunny and hot, only one-hundred and twelve degrees. Sparks had no difficulty convincing his boss of the death of his mother. He reserved a seat on the afternoon flight to Phoenix and got ready to go.

True to their word, the two officers were waiting at the Phoenix airport when Sparks arrived.

They drove directly to the movie set and Sparks started right to work. He installed the receiver in the Cessna in less than fifteen minutes. Then he hooked up the transmitters in the trailer. That took close to an hour.

"Everything is connected, with the exception of the autopilot disabler. I don't need that for this test anyway."

"Why not, Sparks?"

"Because I want whichever one of you who goes up for the test flight to be able to recover if anything goes wrong."

"Sounds reasonable to me, Jim," Charlie said.

Jim and Charlie drew straws to see who would take the plane up; Jim lost. He went and got into the plane while Sparks and Charlie warmed up the transmitter.

Jim started the Cessna up and tuned his radio to an unused frequency. They didn't want anyone to hear what was going on. He taxied out of the barn and stopped. Sparks stood there watching until Jim gave him the thumbs-up signal that the plane was ready. Sparks switched the autopilot override and tried the controls. He made the rudder turn in both directions; the ailerons go up and down. He varied the flap settings. He held the brakes locked and revved up the engine.

"Ok Jim, Charlie is going to take her up. Just sit back, relax, and enjoy the ride," Sparks said into the radio.

Charlie skillfully worked the controls and got the Cessna airborne. He circled the field a couple of times and then brought it in for a landing.

"That was very good, Charlie," Sparks said. "Now let's see if we can put it into the manual override circuit."

Sparks went to work and made a few modifications. Once completed, they were ready to launch the plane again, this time without a passenger. Charlie wanted to see what effect, if any, the jammers would have on it as well as how far away they could control it.

Jim turned on one of the jammers. He raised the antenna on the roof of the trailer.

Charlie started the Cessna's engine by remote control. Jim was jamming all of the frequencies except for the one that they were operating on. Charlie guided the Cessna to its take-off position. He locked the brakes and tried the controls. Everything responded perfectly.

Charlie revved up the engine and released the brakes. The little plane lurched forward and took to the air flawlessly. He flew the plane in gradually enlarging circles. With each revolution he would increase the distance from the barn and the altitude as well. The little plane responded perfectly.

Jim switched on the cameras. The monitors in the trailer clearly showed the area around the plane as well as the cockpit. Everything was working exactly as it should. Sparks was pleased and convinced of this receiver's reliability.

Charlie brought the Cessna back. Sparks exchanged the receivers and they started all over again. Charlie wanted to test the range of the transmitter, but Jim argued that it wasn't safe without one of them in the plane. What would happen if they got to the end of their range and couldn't return the plane? Charlie finally agreed. Jim could go up on the next test flight and Charlie would test the range of their equipment. The three decided that this would be the last flight of the day and that if all went well the next day there wouldn't need to be any more test flights. Charlie turned the Cessna around and started flying it back to them.

Meanwhile, at Nellis Air Force Base in Nevada, the 11th Reconnaissance Squadron was testing one of its latest models of the Predator Unmanned Aerial Vehicle. The Predator, a 27-foot long unmanned aircraft, can fly around over a target for up to 40 hours at altitudes up to twenty-five thousand feet and provide real-time imagery via satellite to commanders on the ground. They were having problems with some sort of electronic interference that seemed to be coming from the southeast. Several times the Predator had, inexplicably, started to fly around in circles; its cameras had turned on for a short time and then turned off. All of their attempts to regain control of it were unsuccessful. Then, it flew southeast for several miles and suddenly landed in the middle of a road and shut itself off. The squadron commander requested the National Military Command Center (NMCC) task a satellite to photograph the area and try to determine the source of the interference.

The Officer of the Day at the NMCC took the request and hand-carried it to his superior. The tasking request was granted and the order to change the satellite was given. The satellite, however, would not be in position to look at that area for another four and a half minutes.

In the desert, Charlie brought the little plane in for a flawless landing. He taxied it into the barn and shut off the engine. Jim began turning off switches of the equipment in the trailer and he lowered the antenna.

Thousands of miles in space, a satellite passed over an area of the Earth where it was instructed to turn on its cameras and other equipment that would be able to sense electronic signals. It did not pick up any unusual electronic signals. All it got were pictures of the Arizona desert and some buildings and a semi parked near them. It would take the Photographic Intelligence guys a few hours to analyze the photos but the initial take was that there was nothing there that could cause the problems they were experiencing. The initial report was sent down the line.

Meanwhile, at Nellis Air Force Base, the operator who had initially reported the interference saw his screens clear up and could find no trace of the problems he had been having. He was finally able to restart the Predator and fly it back to base. He reported this to his superior as well.

"Sparks," Jim began as they pulled the doors of the barn closed, "you are an absolute genius when it comes to remote control airplanes. I do have a question, though. How are you going to rig a truck?"

"Oh, that's even easier than a plane, Jim," Sparks said with a gleam in his eye. "The first thing that I have to do is to find a truck with a manual transmission. By electronically bypassing the key-switch, with the truck in first gear, I just start it up and let it do the rest. The newer vehicles all have locked steering wheels that only unlock when the key switch is turned. It's really quite simple."

"And beautiful in its simplicity too, Sparks."

"Yes, but," Charlie interjected, "what happens if someone with a key tries to take the truck somewhere else?"

"They won't be able to, Charlie, because part of my setup requires me to interrupt the normal starting wiring. All that would happen when they turn the key is the idiot lights on the dashboard would come on and then nothing, just like a dead battery."

Sparks went on to explain that his plan was almost perfect in that the only way for someone to move the truck would be to tow it. He would install a Mercury switch that would sense if the truck were lifted up to an angle of more than 5 degrees. If that happened it would detonate the explosives, once he activated everything. He also planned to place other vehicles or equipment around it to make it less appealing for anyone to try to move it.

The three men went to bed early that night. It had been a very busy day, and another was awaiting them in the morning.

At breakfast the next morning, Charlie suggested that Jim and Sparks fly the Cessna back to Orange County with the receiver for the 747. In that way they could also test the range of the transmitter at the same time.

Shortly after breakfast the three men went out to the barn. They had already agreed that if this test flight went well they would go ahead with the plan in one week. They would pick a Saturday morning flight. Charlie said that he would put an ad in the Los Angeles Times "Personals" column saying "looking for the Sparks to fly" if they were ready to go; Sparks agreed. It was also decided that Sparks would send them a signal, by turning the Cessna's cameras on and then off twice if they needed to abort the mission.

"How will we know what flight we're taking over or what time of day?" Jim asked.

"I've installed a light on the control console in the trailer that will come on when the auto-pilot bypass takes over. When you see the light come on, throw this switch to disable the planes manual controls and give you full control of the plane. By listening to the tower's radio you'll be able to pick up the flight number."

"All right then," Boyle said, "the two of you get going back to L.A."

The two men loaded the receiver into the Cessna and prepared to take-off.

Their flight back to Los Angeles went perfectly. Charlie did everything

from the trailer parked in the desert. Jim and Sparks just sat back and watched. Jim radioed the tower for landing clearance, but Charlie did all of the flying. The three men were very happy to see just how well everything went.

What the three men did not know was that a Predator drone, which had been flying over Nellis Air Force Base, had left its assigned area and was flying a parallel course toward Los Angeles. With every command that Charlie gave the Cessna, the Predator copied. Once the Cessna landed the Predator did too, right in the middle of the Hollywood freeway.

As soon as they landed in Los Angeles, Sparks got out of the plane, took his package, and left the airport. He did not want to be seen near the small plane if possible.

Charlie, at the controls, turned the Cessna around promptly and flew it back to the desert. The whole flight was perfect, from beginning to end. Everything performed exactly as planned.

When Jim got back to the desert hideout with the little plane, Charlie drove into town and made a telephone call to the Los Angeles Times office and placed a personal ad, to run for four days. It read, "Go Sparky Go. Good Luck, C!"

Two days later there was a personal ad in the Phoenix paper that said "J. I'll see you Saturday at 10 a.m., S"

"Okay Jim, we're on for Saturday," Charlie said, "We'd better get the Cessna back to L. A. this afternoon."

"Roger that, Charlie; I'll leave right now and that way I should be there in time to catch a flight back to Phoenix tonight. You can pick me up in Phoenix."

"But, aren't you afraid to fly commercial? After all you might get skyjacked."

The two men laughed heartily, and then Jim added, "No, I'll take a different airline."

The two men walked out to the barn and rolled the small plane outside. Jim climbed inside and started it up.

"I'll see you tonight, in Phoenix," Jim said, as he taxied away. Jim flew directly to the Los Angeles International Airport. He taxied over to an area where small planes were assigned. He paid cash for one week's parking. He ordered the fuel tanks filled, and said that he would be in town on business for a few days.

He left the parking area quickly and went to the ticket counter of one of the other airlines and purchased a one-way ticket to Phoenix. He made no attempt to contact Sparks. From this moment on, it was just a matter of time. If all went well, they would be very rich in one week.

Jim got on the flight back to Phoenix when the gate agent made the announcement. The flight was smooth and quiet. Charlie met him at the airport, and they drove back to the desert, to wait for Saturday.

CHAPTER ELEVEN

Early Saturday morning Jim and Charlie got up, had breakfast and got set to go. The Cessna was parked, inconspicuously, amongst the other small airplanes at Los Angeles International airport. Jim got behind the wheel of the semi and drove it to Yuma, to a truck stop just outside the city. Charlie was in the trailer, warming up the equipment. The only thing left was for them to get the signal from Sparks that the 747 had actually taken off.

Sparks worked the graveyard shift that day, from midnight Friday till eight o'clock Saturday morning. He had traded shifts with a co-worker on the pretense that he wanted to go away for the weekend. He had plenty of time to install the receiver in the plane without being seen. The airport truck was also ready and standing by. He had taken the keys out of it and hid them so that no one would try to move it. He had taken the small wire that connects the solenoid to the key switch and cut it. Then he connected the two halves to a small relay switch that was controlled by a remote control receiver. Then he put a suitcase, containing explosives and a detonator, in back of the seat.

Once the truck was ready, Sparks drove it to the spot, which he had selected, about fifteen feet away from the southeast concourse. Just outside the door leading to one of the gate ramps. Then he took the keys and dropped them down a sewer.

In the airport, at nine thirty, the passengers were checking in and preparing to go on board the plane. The pilot, Joshua Smith, and his co-pilot, Bob Underwood, were going over their preflight checklists, checking both the outside of the plane and the cockpit controls.

Captain Smith called the tower to check his radio, and told them that everything looked okay for take-off.

"Flight Twelve to New York's John F. Kennedy International Airport is now available for boarding at gate sixty-four in the southeast concourse. All passengers with confirmed tickets may now report to gate sixty-four for boarding," a soft feminine voice announced over the loud speaker.

The excited passengers began to move through the gate and onto the plane. The security people had already screened them to make sure that no one had weapons in their pockets, purses, or carry on bags. Shoes had been screened for explosives and Ids checked.

There were three hundred and seventy-five passengers booked for this flight. No one could say so but there were even two, armed air marshals on board. This was the most popular time of day for traveling east.

As the passengers were boarding the jumbo jet, the flight attendants were very busy helping people put their things into the storage bins overhead and showing people where their seats were.

There were four young children on the flight, without their parents; they had to be personally supervised by a flight attendant at all times.

As the last passenger got on board and the door was shut, everything settled down to a relative calm. The flight attendants went about checking to see that everyone's seat belts were fastened and that no one was smoking or talking on a cell phone. The lead attendant made her standard announcements about the oxygen system, the location of the escape hatches, the seat cushions for flotation. She assured the passengers as she went along that it would be highly unlikely to need them.

As the plane was pushed back from the gate, Sparks was watching from his car, near the maintenance hanger.

Once the plane had taxied out to the end of the runway and was waiting for clearance to take-off, the co-pilot informed the pilot that there seemed to be a problem with one of the fuel gauges.

"Number three's fire suppression light won't turn off, skipper," he said, "I've tried resetting the breaker but it won't go out."

"Ok, I'd better call it in."

Captain Smith called the tower and reported the problem. He was instructed to return to the gate and wait for maintenance to arrive.

Captain Smith spoke to the passengers over the intercom.

"Ladies and gentlemen, this is your captain speaking. I am sorry to have to inform you that we are returning to the gate to allow maintenance to fix a problem we are experiencing here on the flight deck. We don't expect a long delay but I will keep you informed. Thank you for your patience."

When Sparks saw the jumbo jet returning to the terminal he became concerned. What kind of problem had they encountered? Could they, somehow, have discovered the remote control receiver? What if they had to take that plane out of service and used a different plane? His palms began to get sweaty and he was getting butterflies in his stomach. All he could do was to sit and watch.

When the 747 returned to the terminal and the maintenance men arrived, Captain Smith was informed that it would take at least two hours, if a part was even available, to replace the fire suppression sensor. The engine cowling would have to be removed and a mechanic would have to climb into the engine, which would need to be cool enough for him to be able to work inside. It was decided that the passengers should deplane and wait inside the terminal, in case it took longer than two hours.

Once again Captain Smith spoke to the passengers over the intercom, "Ladies and gentlemen, I've been in contact with the maintenance people and they have advised me that it will take a minimum of two hours for them to fix our mechanical problem. We've decided, therefore, that it would be best for all concerned if all passengers would deplane and wait inside the terminal. We will announce re-boarding when we have been cleared by the maintenance staff. You may feel free to leave your carry-on luggage on board. Thank you."

The flight attendants opened the door, once the jet way was at the door. They waited patiently as the passengers deplaned and then went into the terminal as well.

Once the passengers were all off loaded, one maintenance man went on board while two others towed a rolling staircase up to the engine. Sparks watched as they removed the engine cowling; he was somewhat relieved that they didn't head for the avionics access panel.

Sparks couldn't decide whether to go back to the avionics shop or continue on toward the desert. He had no way of knowing what was wrong or how long it would take to fix the plane. He had the cell phone number that Jim had given him but he didn't want to use it unless it became really necessary. He finally decided to go back to the shop. He could tell anyone who might ask that he had forgotten something and came back for it.

Sparks went back to the avionics shop and pretended to be looking for one of his tools. He was feeling hungry and needed an excuse to hang around longer so he headed over to the terminal and went to the food court. It was almost eleven o'clock by the time he found a Burger King and ordered a sandwich, French fries, and a Coke. He took his food and sat at a table near the window so that he could watch what was going on out on the field.

Sparks called the cell phone at noon to let the officers know what the delay was. They had been worried as to why they had not received his signal at ten o'clock, the scheduled departure time. Sparks assured them that he would signal as soon as the plane took off.

It was about a quarter till two in the afternoon before the boarding call came for Flight Twelve.

"Flight Twelve to New York's John F. Kennedy International Airport is now available for boarding at gate sixty-four."

Sparks watched as several people who were seated in the dining area hastily finished their food and left the area, headed toward the gate. He finished his Coke, and headed that way too. When he got to Gate sixty-four, he watched until all of the passengers were on board and then he went back to the avionics shop and his car.

When the doors were closed and locked, and the passengers were all seated and strapped in; Captain Smith spoke to the passengers over the intercom.

"Good morning again, ladies and gentlemen, well actually it is good afternoon I guess, this is Captain Smith speaking. We are terribly sorry for the delay and thank you for your patience. We will be taking off in approximately ten to fifteen minutes. We are number three in line. Flight attendants take your seats for take-off."

Sparks watched from his car, his own excitement mounting with each passing moment.

"Los Angeles Tower, this is twelve-heavy; requesting clearance for take-off, over."

"Roger, twelve-heavy, you are cleared for take-off. Good luck Captain Smith, over."

The jumbo jet roared down the runway as each of its four giant engines got louder and louder. Before long the plane was airborne.

As the big plane's nose wheel lifted off of the ground, Sparks breathed a sigh of relief. When the rest of the wheels were off the ground and were being retracted, Sparks pressed a button on the remote control transmitter to signal Jim and Charlie that the plane had finally lifted off.

On the control panel in the semi, at exactly two o'clock on the dot, a green light went on once, and then went out.

"There's the signal from Sparks, Jim," Charlie said over the intercom. Now all we have to do is sit here waiting for them to go to auto pilot."

Jim got out of the cab and walked around to the back of the trailer. He looked around to be sure that no one was watching, then opened the trailer door and went inside, closing the door behind him.

"How will you know when they go to auto pilot, Charlie?" "Sparks built a circuit that will light this light constantly as soon as the autopilot is engaged. Then all I have to do is throw this switch and the override will take over and the plane is ours. When that happens, we'll contact Sparks and he'll make the first call."

"What if the pilot doesn't go to autopilot right away; how about if he decides not to use it at all?"

"No problem, Jim. If the pilot doesn't go to autopilot in exactly ten minutes from now, I'll throw this switch and do it for him. Sparks has thought of everything. The man is a genius."

Just then the red light, indicating that the pilot had engaged the autopilot, came on and stayed on solidly.

Charlie laughed diabolically when he saw it and quickly flipped the switch for the override. Then, he pressed the button on the transmitter that would signal Sparks of their success.

When Sparks saw the light glowing on his transceiver he started his car and drove out of the parking lot. He drove to a nearby pay phone and stopped. He took the receiver off the hook, covered the mouthpiece with a handkerchief, and dialed the number of the control tower.

When he heard the voice of the air traffic control supervisor on the other end of the line, Sparks spoke sternly into the phone.

"Listen very carefully; I will not repeat this again. This is not a crank call. You have exactly five minutes to clear everyone out of the gate 66 area of Terminal 6 before it is blown up. Do you understand? Your five minutes, exactly, is starting right now."

He did not wait for a response. He hung up.

In the tower a dumbfounded air traffic control supervisor was stunned. He called the number for airport security and relayed the message to them.

"Security, this is Sam Wallace, air traffic control supervisor. We just

received a call from someone who claims that he is going to blow up the gate 66 area of Terminal 6 in five minutes. The caller said that it was not a crank call, and that he would not repeat the warning. That was about forty-five seconds ago."

"Okay Sam, thanks. We'll take care of it," the security officer responded. Almost instantly after the security officer put the phone down, it rang again.

"Security office," he said as he answered it.

"Listen carefully; you just got a call from the tower telling you that I called them. You don't know whether or not to believe it. Your time is passing quickly and there are many lives at stake. Look out your window toward gate number sixty-six; you'll see a blue Ford truck parked just outside the door. In exactly three minutes and forty-five seconds that truck as well as gate number sixty-six will be destroyed. Just do as I tell you and get that area evacuated. If you fail, the blood of a lot of innocent people will be on your hands."

The security officer could see the truck from his window, just as the caller said it was. He didn't want to take any chances, if the threat was real as he suspected, but he didn't want to risk a riot either. In a split second, however, he decided to evacuate. He picked up the microphone.

"Attention in the terminal, please; all persons in the area of gates sixty-four, sixty-five, sixty-six, and sixty-seven of Terminal 6 please evacuate the area immediately. Again, all persons in the area of gates sixty-four, sixty-five, sixty-six, and sixty-seven of Terminal 6, please evacuate the area immediately. All security officers please assist."

When the people heard this announcement and the sternness of the warning, some of them began to run towards other parts of the airport. Others stubbornly refused to move for fear of losing their place in line.

The entire security staff rushed into the area, some to each gate in the threatened area, some to their ultimate doom. They were fervently trying to get people to move to safety, without anyone getting hurt. Even though the ticket agents had left, there were still people insisting that it was a prank or something and refused to leave their place in line.

There was confusion everywhere.

As the last three seconds ticked by on Sparks' watch, he reached down and picked up the small transmitter that lay on the seat next to him. He pressed the button to start the truck's engine. It sprang to life and lurched forward. The truck covered the short distance very quickly. As it crashed into the wall, Sparks pressed the second button, which detonated the explosives in the truck.

The powerful explosion shattered the windows on both sides of the gate area. There was a forty-foot hole in the terminal wall and there was fire and smoke everywhere. The people who had been closest to the area, in the waiting area, screamed, cursed, and tried to run for the front door. There was terror in the air. Dozens of people had been knocked down and trampled by others who were blindly running, trying to escape.

The sprinkler system had been severely damaged by the explosion. There was water spraying out of broken pipes in one section and a raging fire in another. Some of the people who had not heeded the warnings to move were buried under the rubble; many had died from the explosion.

Security officers tried to help as many of the injured as possible. The control tower supervisor called for police and fire support. Crash trucks were dispatched to fight the fires. All air traffic was diverted so that everyone's full attention could be focused on the disaster.

About twenty minutes after the explosion, the Air Traffic Control Supervisor's phone rang again.

"Now that you see that I am no crank, I'll tell you what" the muffled voice said "is next, Twelve-heavy from Los Angeles to New York has just been hijacked, by me. If you do not wish to see the plane and all on board destroyed in mid-air, you must pay ten million dollars in exactly three hours." The phone went dead.

"Has anyone heard anything from twelve-heavy to JFK," he asked.

"Nothing since I talked to him on take off," the attendant responsible for twelve-heavy said.

"Well the guy who called and warned of the bomb threat just called and said that he'd hijacked them."

"Now that's absurd. We haven't heard anything from Captain Smith." "No sense taking chances get him on the radio for me."

"Twelve-heavy this is Los Angeles Tower over"

"Los Angeles this is Twelve-heavy, over"

"Twelve-heavy, we just received a telephone tip that you may be experiencing some kind of difficulty up there, over."

"Negative Los Angeles, we're doing fine, no sign of any problems here. Do you think we should be on the lookout for anything in particular, over?"

"We're not sure. I'll have to get back to you, out."

When the controller finished talking to the pilot, a cautious sigh of relief went up from the crowd, but no one was sure of what would come next; nothing had happened to the plane, at least not yet.

While the tower and the pilot were talking, Charlie and Jim were monitoring their conversation.

"Time to let them in on our little secret, Jim," Charlie said as he turned on the autopilot override.

Charlie gave the jumbo jet's controls a command that put it into a very sharp right hand turn. This caused the right wing to dip sharply, much to the surprise of everyone on board.

Two flight attendants were wheeling carts of drinks down the aisles when it suddenly dropped its right wing and veered to the right. They were thrown across the passenger's compartment head first, followed by their carts. One was killed when the overhead compartment she crashed into broke her neck. Several people, who had been standing at the forward bar, were thrown across the plane too.

The pilot and copilot, both, grabbed for the controls to try to straighten the plane out. They were not successful. The pilot tried to recover manual control, by turning off the autopilot, but to no avail. At last he tried turning off several of the control switches and overrides; nothing worked.

At the same instant, over Nellis Air Force Base, a Predator that was just taking off veered sharply to the right; its right wing tip hit the ground and the drone cart-wheeled onto the runway and burst into flames.

Charlie changed the controls to make the plane turn sharply to the left. Again the plane responded quickly, much to the surprise of all on board. There were people, everywhere. Some injured some dead, some in shock, and some in tears. Three of the four children that were traveling alone had been playing on the spiral staircase in the front of the plane during the first violent turn— two of them were dead and the third had multiple broken bones and contusions. Charlie made several more violent maneuvers with the jumbo jet; too late, Captain Smith turned on the Fasten Seat Belts sign. "Los Angeles this is Twelve-heavy, HELP!" "Twelve-heavy, what's wrong up there?" "I don't know Los Angeles, something or someone has taken control of my plane."

At that point Charlie broke into the radio conversation.

"Good morning, gentlemen. This is the voice of that something. As we told you before, Los Angeles, Twelve-heavy has been hijacked. You have three hours to raise ten million dollars or the plane and all on board will be destroyed in mid-air. Goodbye for now, we will be in touch."

Charlie then flipped the switches on all or the jammers and set their power output to maximum. In a matter of seconds all radar, radio, television, and cell phone communications within a four-hundred mile radius of their location went berserk, except for one, ultra low frequency on which no one except the military was allowed to operate.

"Okay, Jim, let's head for the barn. I'll set the 747 down on that hard packed road near there and we'll see about our money."

At Nellis Air Force Base, pandemonium was breaking out too. The top brass wanted to know what had caused one of their precious Predators to crash. No one seemed to have any kind of an answer and that was totally unacceptable.

Jim climbed down out of the trailer and climbed back up into the cab of the truck. He started the engine and quickly pulled out of the truck stop, headed for the movie set.

Charlie turned the 747 onto a course that would fly it to their desert lair. He slowed its speed down to keep it from arriving too much before they could get there to land it.

Meanwhile, at twenty-five thousand feet, directly over Nellis Air Force Base in Nevada, another Predator drone left its prescribed flight plan; it had performed a sharp right turn followed by a sharp left hand turn before straightening out and heading south, toward Arizona, much to the surprise of its controllers in the van on the ground.

Sparks was in his car, heading toward the desert at the posted speed limit. He didn't want to draw any attention to himself at this point.

Once the 747 was level and flying straight, the pilot made a frightening announcement to his passengers.

"Ladies and gentlemen," he said, trying and failing miserably to remain calm, "this is your captain speaking. I am sorry to report to you that this aircraft has been electronically hijacked. The violent maneuvers of the past several minutes were a demonstration by the individuals on the grounds who have taken control. Therefore, please remain in your seats with your seatbelts securely fastened. I will be coming back to help the injured in a few moments. Only those medically trained personnel on board and members of the crew should be out of their seats. Thank you for your cooperation."

Then the captain got on the intercom phone and called for a flight attendant in first class. All of them had been injured in the incident a few minutes earlier. An air marshal answered the phone and the pilot asked for both air marshals to come to the cockpit so that he could update them.

With the pilot's announcement and the lack of flight crew, there was no one left in the passenger compartments to take charge of the situation. A young intern by the name of Fred Carney was traveling with his new bride to New York and then on to Boston to do his internship at Brigham and Women's hospital was on board. He began trying to treat the injured. A priest offered his services to provide last rights to the dead and dying. Some of the panicked passengers began to calm down when they saw this.

Some of them cursed, some prayed, but all wondered what would happen to them. They were utterly helpless.

The only other medically trained person on board, besides doctor Carney, was a nurse. She quickly began to treat some of the injured. Two of the stewardesses had died, almost instantly, when their necks were broken. There were many broken bones and a lot of cuts and bruises.

One man, on the verge of hysteria, went to the stewardess's phone and began screaming into it for someone to come from the cockpit to help his wife who was in labor.

"Captain, I am one of your passengers. Please get back here right away to help. All of your stewardesses are hurt, two of them are dead I think. There is a doctor on board but he is very busy and my wife is about to have our baby. Pleas help us!" He pleaded sobbing as he slumped to the floor clutching the phone with both hands.

Captain Smith and the co-pilot both went back to the passenger compartments. They couldn't be of use in the cockpit anymore.

The first order of business was to restore some kind of order out of the pandemonium so that no one else got hurt. The last thing they needed was a riot. The second would be to help the injured and the pregnant woman as best they could.

The scene, in the passenger compartment, that greeted them as they came out of the cockpit was worse than either of them had imagined. There were people lying all over the place, the drink carts were twisted and smashed on top of some of the victims. There was broken glass, blood, and spilled drinks everywhere.

"Is there anyone on board who has been trained for First Aid?" the captain shouted.

Two young boys, who were splinting their father's broken arm, were the only ones who replied.

"We're both working on our First Aid merit badges in the Boy Scouts." "Well, help here and I'll personally see that you get those badges," Joshua softly replied.

When the two boys finished with their father's arm they began to treat some of the other passengers whose injuries were not too severe.

The nurse, by this time, had gotten back to the woman in labor. The trauma had triggered a miscarriage. There was not much she could do for the woman because there were no drugs available and very few medical supplies.

By the time the pilot was able to get to the nurse, she was trying to stop the bleeding of an arterial wound that one of the stewardesses had received. He had seen all of the injured, and he felt totally useless.

Captain Smith picked up the stewardess' phone and called the navigator. "Anything from the hijackers yet, Bob," he asked.

"No, nothing yet and I can't get through on the radio to anyone else either. Looks like their jamming everything. I even tried my cell phone, nothing. We are in some real big trouble."

"You don't know the half of it, Bob. Everything back here is a shambles; we've got two confirmed dead and many more injured and either dead or dying. A lot of them will die if they don't get help soon. Keep trying to get through on the radio;

don't stop for any reason. Meanwhile we'll stay back here and do what little we can.

Between the two officers, the doctor, the nurse, and the Boy Scouts most of the injured got some type of aid. The severely injured were left to the doctor and the nurse. The biggest problem was the lack of sufficient medical supplies. The First Aid kits on the plane were not stocked for this type of emergency.

The pilot asked for men who had white shirts on to turn them in to be used as bandages. Blankets were ripped into strips to be used as splint ties. Business men's ties were also collected for tourniquets.

"Captain, we don't have any disinfectant left," the nurse called.

"Use whiskey or anything from the bar and drink carts that aren't broken."

On the ground, Jim had turned the tractor trailer off of the main road and into the movie lot. The 747 was directly overhead.

Charlie opened up the radio frequency that he had used earlier to communicate with the plane. He was careful; however, to adjust the jammers in such a way that only the plane's pilot could receive the message.

"Twelve-heavy, do you read me, over?"

"This is Twelve-heavy. I read you loud and clear, over."

"We are going to land your plane. You are not to try to get out. I repeat no one is to leave your aircraft. Anyone who does will be shot and then we will blow up the plane with every one on board. Do not attempt to contact any one either. Is that understood?"

"We understand you perfectly, but what about our injured? We need a doctor and medical supplies. We have over a hundred people who were injured when you turned us around."

"That is too bad. We don't have a doctor. I can't very well go and get one either. You'll have to do the best that you can on your own."

The navigator used the intercom to announce that they were going to land.

"I've received word that we are going to land in just a few minutes, ladies and gentlemen. The hijackers have warned that no one is to leave the airplane. Any attempt to leave the plane would result in that person being shot and the rest of us being blown up. Captain Smith, please return to the cockpit. All passengers and other crew members please be seated and fasten your seatbelts it could be a rough landing.

The pilot started forward. As he did, the plane began a slow right turn.

Boyle brought the jumbo jet slowly around and into the wind. He pressed the button to lower the wheels. The remote controls were working perfectly; the wheels came down and locked into place. He raised the airbrakes and lowered the flaps; the big plane slowed noticeably and began to descend.

The Predator was over the Grand Canyon when Charlie Boyle put the

747 into a slow right turn; the Predator went into a slow right turn. Then its wheels lowered and its flaps extended. It landed right at the very lip of the canyon and shut down its engine.

The 747 landed roughly; the desert floor was a lot different than a concrete runway. The big plane bounced along but finally came to a halt; six of its tires had blown out as it bounced on the desert floor. Joshua Smith knew that whoever was at the controls was a very good pilot.

Once the landing was complete, Charlie taxied the plane over to a spot that he and Jim had gotten ready for this moment. As soon as the plane was in position Charlie turned off its four big engines and all of its power, except lights, radio, and air-conditioning. The plane was now even more totally helpless. Even if and when they were released, the flight crew could not restart the engines to leave.

Charlie and Jim drove over to the plane in the movie car. They got out and went to a small pile of brown canvass bags that lay nearby.

Methodically, the two officers unpacked the camouflage netting they had always carried in the cargo hold of the A-3. It would work very nicely to hide the 747 from nosy eyes in the sky. It would just look like a sand dune on the desert floor.

Once they covered the plane, Charlie went back to the trailer. Jim stayed with the plane. He carried an M-16 and a thirty-eight caliber pistol. Jim was there to make sure that no one left the plane. He positioned himself so that he was clearly visible to the people inside.

Charlie turned off the plane's power, even the lights and air-conditioner. He wanted to be sure that no attempt could be made to contact the outside world, once he lowered the jamming net.

Charlie switched off the jammers. He listened as, slowly, normal radio transmissions resumed. He heard the air traffic controller from Los Angeles call Twelve-heavy. There was no reply from the airliner.

Sparks, in his car driving toward the desert, heard the return of normal transmission too. The announcer on his car radio began trying to explain what had happened to their broadcast. Life, for some people, was beginning to get back to normal. Sparks smiled. By hearing the commercial radio stations getting back on the air, Sparks knew that Charlie and Jim had been successful if getting the jumbo jet on the ground; now for the next phase of their plan.

By the time Sparks got to the desert hide-out it was time to get the ransom money from the airline.

The board of directors of the airlines had held an emergency meeting and decided to pay the ransom. The only problem was where to come up with that much cash in the allotted time. The F.B.I. had tried desperately to discourage them from paying it but they would not be swayed, passenger's lives were at stake.

CHAPTER TWELVE

While the radar had been blacked out, the F.B.I. field office in Nevada had been alerted of the hijacking and the possible need for assistance from the Air Force at Nellis Air Force Base. The people at Nellis were testing a new unmanned drone. It was highly classified and a very closely guarded secret; it was equipped with lots of modern accessories like thermal imaging and look-down radar that was supposed to be able to "see" through things, including several feet of solid earth. It was still being tested but from what little the F.B.I. had heard about it, it should be able to help provided the Air Force would allow it.

The senior field agent from the Las Vegas office, Joe Brown drove to the air base and requested to see the commandant. His credentials got him right in.

Agent Brown, a man of impeccable taste, wore a gray Brooks Brothers suit, a navy blue silk tie, and a pair of highly polished Stetson shoes. His hair was trimmed to a perfect flat-top, his nails were even manicured. He was escorted into Major General Frederick J. Wainright's office by the general's aide, Major Frank Briggs.

"General Wainright, this is Special Agent Joe Brown of the Las Vegas office of the F.B.I.," he said.

Major General Frederick J. Wainright looked Agent Brown up and down, as if inspecting an enlisted man. The scowl on his craggy face made Agent Brown nervous.

"What can I do for the Federal Bureau of Investigation, Agent Brown," the general asked motioning to a chair across from his desk.

Agent Brown related the story of the hijacking and exactly what it was that was being requested.

"General, what we need is for you to send your unmanned drone up to scour the area for a 747 full of people that have no ability to contact us. We have no idea where it is, only that it was taken by some hijackers. We know where it was headed, we know when and approximately where it was taken but that is all we know. We assume that in the time between when it was taken and when we where notified that the radar and communication blackout ended it could have gotten to Nevada, Arizona, New Mexico, or even old Mexico. We just don't know. Will you help?"

General Wainright was livid that the secrecy surrounding the Predator program had been violated. He demanded to know how the F.B.I. had found out about the program. Agent Brown was not aware of the details surrounding the gathering of the information and attempted to divert the general's anger away from himself. He suggested that General Wainright call the Pentagon.

The general ordered his aide to get the Pentagon on the phone. He was put through to the Secretary of the Air Force's office quickly.

"This is Major General Frederick J. Wainright, commander of Nellis Air Force Base in Nevada, Mister Secretary," he said. "I have an agent from the F.B.I. here in my office asking questions about our Top Secret Predator Project. He is asking for our assistance, sir. I am very concerned about the breach of security that allowed the F.B.I. access to the information that the project even exists."

Agent Brown could not hear the other side of the conversation but he could tell by the change in General Wainright's facial expressions that he his mood was not going to change for the better. After several "Yes sirs" and "No sirs" General Wainright hung up the phone. Agent Brown had guessed right.

"I don't know who, how, or why you fellows at the bureau found out about this project. I bust my ass daily to keep security high and tight around here and someone in Washington takes it upon themselves to blab everything. I don't like it one bit but I've been ordered to assist you in what ever way I can."

Agent Brown did his best to calm the general down and again explained that a 747 with more than three hundred people on board had been hijacked and was being held for ransom. He asked if the Air Force could task one of its drones, that was the only thing he had heard them called, could search for it.

General Wainright told Agent Brown about the unexplained crash of one of the Predators and the mysterious actions of the second Predator. The times of the incidents seemed familiar to Agent Brown. He checked his notes and realized that the Predator crash happened at about the same time as the radar problem had gone away. He pointed that detail out to the general.

General Wainright agreed to provide one of the remaining Predators for the task. It had thermal imaging and look-down radar as well as realtime satellite communication with his command center. It would be launched in approximately two hours. It was to fly over an area to the south of Nellis, over the Arizona desert. Another Predator would be held in reserve to go up if, and when it became necessary.

CHAPTER THIRTEEN

Charlie turned his transmitter to a frequency that was different than the one he had contacted the airport tower previously. He didn't want anyone to trace him if possible.

"Los Angeles Tower, this is Twelve-heavy, over."

"Twelve-heavy this is Los Angeles tower, where are you, over?"

"Don't worry about that, Los Angeles; the question is where my money is?"

One of the F.B.I. agents walked over and took the microphone. "Twelve-heavy, or who ever you are, this is Special Agent Fred Barns of the Federal Bureau of Investigation. I want to know who you are and why you are doing this, over."

"In answer to your question let me just say this. I have Twelve-heavy and over three hundred passengers. Unless you want them all blown straight to hell, and I think you know by now that I can and will do what I say, you'd better pay up. I want ten million dollars in exactly ten minutes or you can kiss them all good bye. Or perhaps you'd prefer another demonstration there."

Charlie was just bluffing; they didn't really have another demonstration ready at the airport. He knew it, so did Sparks and Jim, but the F.B.I. didn't know.

"Okay, you win. The airline has agreed to pay, but only after you prove that you haven't blown up the plane already."

Boyle turned on the plane's radio power on again. He called Captain Smith on the radio.

"Captain, this is your captor speaking. I have the F.B.I. on the radio. I want you to tell them that you are alive. Tell them anything you like, except where you are. I want you to let them know that we haven't blown up your airplane, yet."

The ominous sound of Charlie's voice made it clear to Captain Smith that he'd better sound convincing.

The captured pilot was careful to tell the F.B.I. agent exactly who he was, what had happened, and of the condition of his passengers and crew.

"We need a doctor desperately. I have several people who will die if they don't get help soon. I don't know what to do for..."

Charlie turned off the plane's power and the radio was again silent for a moment.

"This is Special Agent Barns. What do you want me to do with the money?"

Charlie told Agent Barns that there would be a pilot-less plane to pick up the money.

"You are not to attempt to follow this plane in anyway. If you do, I'll blow up the 747. Put only the money in the plane. Do not try any tricks and do not attempt to sneak anyone aboard the plane. If you comply you will save the lives of more than three hundred people. If you don't they will all die. Do you understand?"

"Yes, I do. No one will attempt to follow and there will be no tricks. You have my word."

"You have ten minutes."

Charlie switched off the transmitter. He went to the main console along the side wall of the trailer; the television monitors were showing only snowy screens. He turned on the remote controls for cameras on the small plane; all six monitors came on and he could clearly see all around the Cessna. The cameras in the wing tips gave him a view of both sides. The cameras in the tail and nose gave him front and rear vision. The cockpit camera allowed him to see the entire interior of the plane and the belly camera enabled him to see all around the lower part of the plane.

Once he checked out all of the cameras, Charlie started the little plane's engine and taxied it away from the other small planes.

Charlie could see the surprised look on the faces of several people standing nearby as the little plane began to move with out a pilot.

Charlie called the tower once again.

"You will see a small plane coming towards you. When it stops, one person only may approach it. Open the pilot's door and put the money in the back seat. Don't try any tricks. I can see every move you make. Do exactly as I say and nothing will happen."

Charlie watched the monitors as he taxied the Cessna to the base of the tower. He stopped it right in front of a small ground level door. This door led directly to the tower. He watched as a well-dressed man, carrying a suitcase, approached the plane. The man walked to the door of the plane and opened it. The man, Special Agent Barns looked directly into the camera. He placed the suitcase on the backseat of the plane just as Charlie had told him to do. He closed the door and backed slowly away from the Cessna.

Charlie watched the monitors intently. He rotated the cockpit and belly cameras to make sure that no one had tried to sneak aboard the plane.

Charlie turned on the jammers. They were set to jam everything except the frequency at which the remote control receiver was working. The cameras were multiplexed onto the same frequency as well.

The engine on the little plane sped up and taxied away from the tower. He turned it to the far end of a runway and turned it into the wind for take-off.

The little plane moved quickly down the runway and into the air. Charlie made it climb to an altitude of fifteen hundred feet and flew it at maximum speed, directly out to sea.

Once he had the plane away from the watchful eyes of Los Angeles. He turned it toward the desert.

Over the Arizona desert, a lone Predator started to fly in erratic and irregular turns, as if it were following a road; suddenly its engine roared to maximum power and it began to climb sharply. The Predator's camera and look-down radar came to life; the controller could see everything that the Predator saw. It finally turned to the southeast and flew in a straight line; totally out of Air Force controller's hands.

Jim had come into the trailer after Sparks had arrived and was busy watching the monitors for any signs that the little plane was being followed.

The Cessna was heading east for less than twenty minutes when Jim noticed a spot on the screen. It was barely visible but he could see it. The little plane was being followed.

"Charlie, take a look at the tail monitor. I think we're being followed."

Charlie stared intently at the monitor. He turned the camera on the belly around and focused it on the object as well. He was certain that they were being followed. It looked like a helicopter.

Charlie turned the Cessna around and flew it straight for the object. It was a helicopter, from one of the Los Angeles television stations.

"Jim, get on the radio and tell those idiots to get that chopper out of there. Don't open everything up though. Just give them one frequency."

"Right, Charlie."

Jim reduced the power on one of the jammers. This allowed him to radio the tower. He told them of the helicopter and warned them to get it out of there.

"We tried to stop them before they left. They insisted that it was their right to follow the story."

Charlie got on the radio and was very stern. He warned that if they didn't leave, or be shot down he would kill all of the people on the 747.

The F.B.I. tried pleading, ordering, and cajoling the helicopter crew to turn back or be fired upon. They continued to be defiant and claim their constitutional right to follow the story even if it meant the deaths of more than three hundred people.

Within five minutes an Air Force F-16 fighter flew past the Cessna and approached the helicopter. The fighter pilot warned the helicopter to turn back or be fired upon. The helicopter pilot again refused and was immediately shot down with a short burst of twenty millimeter cannon fire. The fighter turned back towards Nellis Air Force Base and disappeared from sight.

Once Charlie and Jim were convinced that they were no longer being followed, Charlie returned the Cessna's controls to the original course and altitude. He flew the plane directly to their hide-out. He landed the plane easily on the desert floor and taxied it into the barn.

The Predator turned back toward Nellis for a short time and then, just as inexplicably it turned back to the southeast. It flew directly toward the desert hide-out of the hijackers; the Air Force controller had no idea where it was going. The hijackers had no idea that the Predator was near them; but, the Air Force operator saw the image of the jumbo jet from the look-down radar and he could see the images of a large number of people from a thermal scan of the plane. He reported these findings to his superiors, along with their latitude and longitude. At Nellis Air Force base, the pictures were sent, by secure land-line communications to FBI headquarters in Washington where they were relayed to Los Angeles. This all took less than two minutes. The order went out from the Pentagon to sit tight until the hijackers tried to leave that area. No chances were being taken that might spook the hijackers and cause them to destroy the passengers of the downed airliner. A flight of four F-16 Eagles were scrambled and told to circle the Air Force base until they received further instructions.

As soon as the Cessna was in the barn, Charlie turned off the engine. Jim closed the barn doors and then went to the small plane and removed the suitcase containing the money. He carried it to the back of the semi where Charlie met him and together they examined the stacks of money. They couldn't find any die packs, explosives, or transmitters. They were satisfied that their demands had been met completely.

"Jim, set the self-destruct timer for one hour. I've set all of the jammers to maximum power and range. I'll get Sparks and we'll get out of here. My guess is that they'll be doing a satellite thermal scan of this area to try to track the heat trail left by the Cessna. That will probably give us less than an hour to get clear of here before they can get a fix on our position."

Jim went right to work. He placed all of the charges and set the timer dial to sixty minutes. The timer would set off the blasting caps which would ignite the C-4 explosives that he had placed in the trailer, the Cessna, the jammers, and everything they had touched.

Charlie climbed aboard the stolen Navy jet and started the engines. Except for the shape of the airplane everything that they could have done to disguise it had been done by painting it and removing some of the external hardware; it no longer looked like a military aircraft. Jim placed the suitcase of money in the crew's compartment. Sparks was busy pouring gasoline on the Cessna, the cars, the motorcycle and everything that he could reach in the barn. Jim had parked the semi right next to the barn. Close enough to set the barn on fire if the explosives failed to do so.

As soon as everything was done the men locked the barn doors and the back of the trailer and they climbed aboard their plane. Charlie pushed the throttles all of the way forward as soon as they were aboard. Within seconds they were airborne and headed south toward Mexico; the A-3 climbed to thirteen thousand feet, well below the ever seeing Predator.

The drone recorded the liftoff and their course and speed. Within minutes the flight of four F-16 fighters was ordered to follow the A-3. They were followed by two C-130 cargo planes that were headed toward the downed airliner.

As the A-3 headed toward the Mexican border, under a cloud of radar blackout, the three men wondered if they would ever be able to see their beloved country again. They were now fugitives, or would be if no one had seen them or figured out that they were still alive, or if, if what? They had tried to think of every possible contingency; this was, after all, a military operation and it had been planned as such.

It took them most of and hour to get to the Mexican border because Charlie would fly south, then west, then north, then south again. Trying to make sure no one was following them. They were impeded, after all, by the same radar blackout as everyone else was. They had no idea that the Predator was overhead, reporting their every move. This also gave the F-16's time to overtake them and devise a plan to take them down.

Back in the Arizona, the pilot of the downed 747 heard the A-3 take off. He was not able to see it because of the camouflage netting that covered his aircraft.

Once the sound of the jet engines had diminished and he was sure that the plane had gone, Captain Smith went back into the passenger's compartment. The large, inflatable escape chute began filling up and the passengers started to stir.

"Ladies and gentlemen," he shouted, "please listen to me. I believe that our captors have just flown off in the plane we just heard taking off. I can not be certain, however, that they are all gone. Please stay inside until I return."

"Bob," he called to the co-pilot, "you stand in this door until I return. For God's sake, don't let anyone leave."

With that he jumped into the escape chute and slid to the ground. Once outside, he was not sure which way to go. He was disoriented by the heat and the bright sunlight. He had no way of knowing that he was less than a mile away from the barn and his own explosive death.

The desert winds moved the sands around on the land in front of him, behind him, and all around him. He hadn't gone very far until he was totally lost in the blowing sand. He did, however see one foot print, headed away from where he was standing. He started to head in that direction. A large piece of sagebrush, swept along by the wind, flew into his face and knocked him to the ground. As he was getting to his feet, he caught a glimpse of what looked like a building in the distance. He wasn't sure how far away it was but he slowly started in that direction. He moved slowly and deliberately in that general direction, stopping frequently to try to catch a glimpse of life but he never saw anyone.

About this time, Captain Smith was joined by one of the passengers, Mister Samuel James.

"What are you doing here?" The pilot asked. "I told everyone to stay aboard. How did you get past the co-pilot?

"I snuck up behind him and hit him and knocked him down and then jumped out. I've been cooped up in that plane for too long. I'd rather join you out here and take my chances."

"Well listen up, and listen good. There is a building of some kind ahead. It could be their hide out. I can't be sure that they are all gone so stay close to the ground and don't make a sound. I don't want to lose anymore of my passengers."

The two men moved slowly. They crouched low and moved cautiously, pausing frequently to watch for any signs of movement.

They had gotten to a spot less than a hundred yards from the building before they could really make out the shape and size of the building. It was an old barn and there was a tractor-trailer truck parked right next to it.

It seemed too quiet. Could it be that their captors had truly left? Could they be coming back? Neither man knew the answer. They found out, too late. Approximately three minutes later, the silence was totally blocked out by a tremendously violent explosion and a blinding bright flash of light. Neither man saw the flash; they were killed by flying debris from the truck and trailer. The Predator did.

The passengers and crew aboard the 747 heard the blast and the explosion. No one knew the fate of their captain but there were a lot of terrified passengers; they could hear debris falling everywhere.

The co-pilot waited for what seemed like hours, even though it was really only ten minutes, and then called for some of the other passengers to come outside with him and remove the camouflage netting from their aircraft. He took three volunteers and went looking for Captain Smith and Mister James. They walked in the direction of the explosion. It didn't take long for them to find the two men; both were dead. Various wounds covered their bodies. Mister James was missing one arm and part of his face. Captain Smith had been hurt by the blast much worse; he had been decapitated. Both men were a mass of blood and it made all three members of the search party vomit. They could see that the building or what was left of it was ablaze and there had been some vehicles but they were a mass of twisted wreckage now. They turned and went back to the plane.

Bob Underwood called to the navigator and asked him to send down a dozen or so of the able-bodied men to assist him in removing the camouflage netting. Twenty of them came out. They all went to work pulling out the stakes, taking down the supports, and removing as much of the netting as they could reach from the ground. The navigator took several more men and climbed out of the pilot's and copilot's windows and pulled from the top. It took a little more than an hour to uncover the jumbo jet. Before they could finish, the first of the C-130 cargo planes touched town and taxied up to them. The uninjured flight crew opened the doors and released more of the escape chutes and began to evacuate the passengers. The second C-130 landed shortly after the first. After the explosion, all radio reception had resumed. The C-130 pilot, of the first plane on the ground radioed Nellis and requested additional helicopters as well as medics, stretchers, and medical supplies.

The Predator, following the A-3, reported that the plane was nearing the Mexican border. In Washington DC, the Ambassador from Mexico was contacted and asked to come to the White House at his earliest possible convenience; it took him less than thirty minutes to arrive.

The President asked for, and was given, permission to pursue the renegade military aircraft over Mexican soil, and to shoot it down if necessary. The four F-16's were notified and went to afterburner to catch-up and bring down the A-3.

The Predator saw the A-3 turn west, toward the Pacific Ocean. The operator missed the three parachutes descending toward the ground.

It took only forty-five seconds for the F-16's to overtake the A-3. Their attempts to contact the pilot and crew of the wayward jet fell on deaf ears. Several warning shots were fired near the aircraft but went unheeded. The lead pilot radioed for permission to bring the aircraft down. Permission was granted and a heat-seeking missile did the job very quickly.

Charlie, Jim, and Sparks saw the F-16 fire the missile, they were surprised that they had been discovered so soon. They had escaped by a mere minutes; what they didn't realize was that they hadn't totally escaped the eyes in the sky.

The stealth abilities of the Predator, which had proved so useful in the Gulf war, protected it from detection now by the Mexican government. The operator had reviewed the tape of the goings on, after the A-3 had been destroyed. He noticed the parachutes that he had missed previously. He turned the Predator around and followed the path he had previously flown following the plane. It took a little while but he finally saw where the parachutes had gone down. One parachute was caught in a tree, no others were in sight. They were just over the Mexican border. The information was relayed to Nellis, Washington, and Los Angeles.

F.B.I. agents from the Phoenix Field office swarmed all over the 747 and the area around it. They brought in bomb sniffing dogs to try to find the explosives that the hijackers threatened to use if their demands were not met, they found nothing. A team of Air Force medics had been brought in to care for the injured. The critical patients were flown by helicopter to the nearest hospitals. The dead were placed in body bags to be flown back to Los Angeles. The less critical passengers were treated in a hastily constructed field hospital.

The black box, containing the remote control receiver was carefully removed from the airplane and sent to Washington for analysis. Every inch of the plane was checked, rechecked, and rechecked again.

In all, the death count of those who had been aboard was thirty-three. The critically injured numbered another fifty and there were more than a hundred and fifty with minor cuts and abrasions.

CHAPTER FOURTEEN

Sparks had been killed when his parachute was caught in the tree; he was impaled on a broken branch which pierced his heart. His neck had been broken too; he died instantly. Jim and Charlie landed about thirty feet apart, in a small clearing in the forest. They cut their friend down from the tree and buried him in the clearing along with their flight suits, boots, guns, and other flight gear. They took the suitcase containing the money and headed out of the forest in the direction that they believed to be south. Neither man had thought to bring along the compass that had been in their survival gear.

They continued to walk for about an hour before they saw any sign of life. There were two men carrying high powered assault rifles who they presumed were hunters from the way they were dressed. When the two men saw Charlie and Jim they turned toward them. It was then that Charlie and Jim realized that neither of them had brought their pistols.

The two men, seeing their suitcase, assumed that Charlie and Jim were tourists who were lost and that they would have a lot of money with them.

The taller of the two, Juan, spoke first, "Buenos tarde, Señors, do you speak Spanish," he asked Jim and Charlie.

"No, Señor, sorry; do you speak English?"

"Si, I speak English."

"We are a couple of tourists and we seem to be lost," Charlie said.

"You two gringos look like Federalies. Are you," asked Jorge. He was shorter than Juan, only five feet tall; he was bald and weighed two hundred and fifty pounds. His unshaven face made him look dirty as did his clothing. He carried an AK-47 semiautomatic assault rifle.

"No, Señor, we are Americans."

"Are you the Americano who we saw parachuting out of that aero plane that blew up a little while ago," Juan asked.

"Oh, no, Señor that must have been the fellows we saw headed back that way," Jim said pointing in the direction that they had just come from. "they seemed like they were in a real big hurry."

"There were three of them," Boyle interjected.

"Si, that is how many parachutes we saw," Jorge said.

"What do you have in the suitcase, gringo," Juan asked.

"Oh, just a change of clothes and some papers for a meeting we are late getting to," Boyle handled the answer.

Boyle got a queasy feeling in the pit of his stomach, these men were just a little too inquisitive. Johnston cast a knowing glance at Charlie; he was feeling a little nervous too.

"Can we offer you some money to guide us out of the forest, Señor, "Jim asked, hoping that the offer might take their minds off of the suitcase?

"Si, you could offer us all of your money, Señor," Jorge said, raising the barrel of his rifle a little bit.

Jim and Charlie each took out their wallets. They showed the men all of the cash that they had there, which only amounted to about three hundred dollars.

"Here, this is all I have, Señor," Jim said handing him his cash. Boyle followed Jim's lead and handed over his cash too.

"Now the suitcase, gringo," Juan said.

"Señor, it just has my clothing and a few papers in it. I will need those when I get out of this forest," Boyle told him.

Jorge raised his rifle and shot both of them through the head. Then Jorge and Juan hastily went through their victim's pockets but found nothing; they took the men's watches as well. When they opened the suitcase, they couldn't believe their eyes. When they saw all of the stacks of one-hundred dollar bills laying there they almost fainted. Neither man had ever had more than a couple of hundred dollars in his life. Now they were rich.

"Juan, we must bury them so that no one will find them."

"Si, Jorge, you better dig fast, those other gringos from the plane might have heard the shots. Why did you have to kill them anyway?"

"They were hiding something; I had a feeling that they were lying." "Si, Señor."

The two men put their rifles against a tree, took out their hunting knives and began digging a shallow grave for the two gringos.

"So, what do you think you will do with your share of the money, Juan?"

"I think I will get good and drunk, Jorge. What about you?"

"I'm going to get good and drunk too and maybe buy me a senorita at the cantina; ha, ha, ha."

Once they had finished digging a grave big enough to hid their two victim's bodies in, they picked up the dead men and threw them into the hole and covered them up. Then they found a fallen tree and they dragged it to the grave and covered it with the tree. Then they quickly closed the suitcase, took their rifles, and left the area.

It was more than twelve years before the remains of Charlie and Jim were found. The Mexican government notified the United States government of the discovery of two skeletons with dog tags around their necks and requested the F.B.I. to fly the remains to Washington. They offered the F.B.I. the opportunity to investigate the scene where they were found but said that only their Federalies would be allowed to make any arrests. Nothing was found of the money or the men who murdered the two airmen.

THE END